Ruskin Bond was born in Kasauli in 1934, and grew up in Jamnagar, Dehradun, New Delhi and Shimla. He lived in England—in Jersey and London—for four years, returning to India in 1955. He is the author of over a hundred novellas, short-story collections, non-fiction books and collections of poetry. Among them are *Lone Fox Dancing*, *The Room on the Roof*, *A Flight of Pigeons*, *The Night Train at Deoli*, *Time Stops at Shamli*, *The Blue Umbrella*, *Rain in the Mountains*, *Tales of Fosterganj* and *A Book of Simple Living*. He received the John Llewellyn Rhys Prize in 1956, the Sahitya Akademi Award in 1993, the Padma Shri in 1999 and the Padma Bhushan in 2014. He lives in Landour, Mussoorie, with his adopted family.

Captain Young's Ghost

Ghostly Tales from
the Indian Hills

RUSKIN BOND

SPEAKING
TIGER

SPEAKING TIGER PUBLISHING PVT. LTD
1381/4, Ansari Road, Daryaganj
New Delhi 110002

First published in India by Speaking Tiger in paperback 2018

ISBN: 978-93-86338-32-7
eISBN: 978-93-86338-30-3

10 9 8 7 6 5 4 3 2 1

Typeset in Minon Pro by Jojy Philip
Printed at Gopsons Papers Ltd.

Contents

Author's Note

No one who has lived in our mountains ever leaves them, at least not in spirit. So if you live in the Indian hills, it is only a matter of time before you meet a ghost. I have met several; the most memorable of them in the hill stations of north India. Something about the air of Mussoorie, Shimla, Lansdowne and other little Himalayan towns encourages ghostly visitations.

This collection contains new stories, a couple derived from my longer works, and old favourites. Most of the older stories first appeared in magazines and newspapers like the *Illustrated Weekly*, *Statesman*, *Deccan Herald*, *Imprint* and *Blackwood's Magazine*. I had not expected them to become so popular that they are being read forty and fifty years after they were written. I have those ghosts to thank!

And in my experience ghosts can indeed be friendly and generous creatures. Even when they are not, they are rarely bloodthirsty or plain evil. After you have survived the initial scare, you can learn to live with them.

As I have done. Late last night, I heard some long dead residents of Ivy Cottage having tea and gossiping in the living room again. They've been doing this every other night, and I usually leave them in peace. But yesterday they interrupted a very pleasant dream, so I called out from my bed, asking them to shut up, and they did.

RUSKIN BOND
Ivy Cottage, Landour
September 2018

Captain Young's Ghost

He walked into the bar with something of a swagger, although this did not disguise a pronounced limp. He looked slightly familiar, but I couldn't quite place him—I have known too many people and I have been around a long time. So when he walked to my table, smiled charmingly, and said, 'You're on your own, I see. Mind if I join you?' I did not say no.

'Please do,' I responded, only too glad to have someone to talk to. It had been raining all day, cold February rain, and now a heavy mist had come up from the valley and covered most of Barlowganj. There were only two or three guests in the old hotel, and I presumed that he was one of them; an elderly, white-haired foreigner, with time on his hands. I, too, had time on my hands. Fed up with my own company, I had come down to Barlowganj for a drink and a meal. I was well into my second martini and looking forward to a third.

'I'll settle for a whiskey,' said the visitor.

'Indian or Scotch?' asked the barman.

'Irish, if you have it.'

'No Irish, sir. Only Scotch.'

'Blind prejudice. So give me a Scotch.'

He settled back in his chair, surveyed the room (which was empty except for a pianist in the far corner, tinkling away), and asked, 'Why do they call this Captain Young's Bar? That's an Irish name. Does he own this place?'

'He's a historical character,' I said. 'One of the founders of Mussoorie.'

'And is he still around?'

'Oh, no. Must have died a hundred years ago. They say his ghost appears occasionally.'

'Did he die here, then?'

'Actually, no. He survived several wars and went home a General. But people know him as Captain Young, and young he was when he first rode up this hill. Came to India as a boy soldier. Took part in the battle for Delhi.'

'You seem to know a lot about him.'

'Well, I'm the local historian,' I said, finishing my martini and ordering another. 'Would you like to know more about him?'

'The man or the ghost?'

'Both, if you like. His ghost isn't very frightening. You can recognize him from his uniform. And his beautiful white horse. And the sword which he always carries. And his cocked hat—looking like the Duke of Wellington! At least that is how people believe he appears on some nights.'

'And was he popular locally?'

'Well, he was popular with his men, his Gurkha soldiers down in Dehradun. He started the first Gurkha regiment. That was after the war with Nepal. The Gurkhas gave the British a hard time. If it's a clear morning tomorrow, you can look down at the valley and see the hill called Kalinga where the great battle took place. The British General, Gillespie, had his head shot away by a cannon ball. But you won't see his ghost. I don't think he'd care to come this way again. But Young survived, and when the war was over he set about recruiting those brave Gurkhas who had survived the British assault. He took the trouble to learn their language and take part in their ceremonies, religious and otherwise. And those Gurkha brigades were to fight almost everywhere—on the frontier, in Afghanistan, in Burma, in Europe during the World Wars, and not many years ago in the Falkland Islands—the Argentinians were terrified of them.'

'Perhaps they saw Young's ghost as well—carrying a kukri as well as a sword.'

'Young always carried a musket. He liked hunting

in these hills. That's what brought him up here—to hunt, and to build a hunting lodge, the first house in Mussoorie. He called it the Mullingar, after his home in Ireland.'

'You certainly know a lot about him. Have another martini.'

'One for the road. And what about you?'

'I'll stick to whiskey. They should keep some Irish whiskey, considering Young was an Irishman…'

'Well, people forget, you see. Maybe that is why he keeps coming back. To remind them. We truly die when we are forgotten.'

The pianist had gone for his dinner. The barman was nodding off in his corner. All was quiet in the barroom. Still night, silent night. Through the windows and glass doors we could see the terrace garden, the mist coming and going, curling and twisting across the lawn. On the next hill the lights of the hill station twinkled fitfully.

There was noise outside, and the barman looked up, looked out at the mist, almost expecting to see something there. I had my back to the windows. My drinking companion was facing them. A look of astonishment spread across his face. His mouth fell slack. He gasped, gone was his sangfroid, his man-of-the-world look of confidence.

I turned to see what they were gaping at.

Out of the mist, out of the tall oaks, across the lawn, a horseman came riding towards us.

He did not come at a canter or a gallop, just a slow, gliding movement, as of a rider in the sky. The poetry of his motion held us enthralled.

'Captain Young,' whispered the barman, and fled from the room.

I opened the doors and stepped outside. The manager and his assistant were soon by my side. We watched as the rider approached. He was wearing a red coat buttoned up to the chin, knee-high boots, and a sword buckled on to his belt. He was also wearing a helmet, which looked more like something from the Middle Ages than the early nineteenth century. The fools.

The apparition, or whatever it was, stopped. Everyone waited. Then he advanced again. And as he did, what had appeared from a distance to be a splendid horse now turned out to be a local pony, and as it approached it slipped on the concrete slabs of the terrace, and its rider tumbled off, his helmet landing at our feet. The rider gave a curse in Hindi, tried to stand up, then subsided into a flower bed.

The uniformed arrival turned out to be old Foster, a long-time resident of Barlowganj, known for his heavy drinking and his claim to be descended from the kings of Scotland.

'Come, get up now, Mr Foster,' said the manager

irritably. 'You were supposed to have your ration of rum *after* the performance, not before.'

The assistant manager turned to me and said, 'Sometimes we engage Mr Foster to appear as Captain Young's ghost—just to entertain the customers. Did you enjoy the performance, sir?'

'Not very,' I said. 'A Scotsman trying to pass of as an Irishman is unlikely to be very convincing.' And I turned to my drinking companion. 'What did you think of it all?'

But my companion was no longer with us.

'Where's the other gentleman?' I asked the barman. 'The one who was drinking with me?'

'He just left,' said the barman. 'Said he'd heard and seen enough nonsense for one evening.'

'A pity. I was beginning to enjoy his company,' I said, and turned my attention to Foster, who was demanding his fee for the evening's entertainment. They gave him a bottle of rum, put him back on his pony and led him away in the direction of his ramshackle cottage.

It was time for me to go. Somewhere, anywhere.

I bade everyone good night and set off on foot up the steep road from verdant Barlowganj to the heights of Landour. It was a long walk, but distances never bother me.

On the way I passed the gate of Wynberg-Allen, an old school that had survived from the days of the Raj.

My old friend, the night-watchman, was awake in his cabin, chatting with a young acquaintance.

'And how is life treating you, Bahadur?' I asked, speaking to him in Gurkhali. 'I hope you don't find the nights too long.'

'Captain Young-sahib?' exclaimed the retired soldier. 'So good to see you. It's been some time since you came this way.'

'I've been travelling,' I said. 'Looking up old friends.'

'On foot, sahib? And you're not in uniform.'

'I thought I would try being a civilian for a change. Needed some distraction. Stay safe and well, old soldier.'

As I passed on, I heard him say to his companion, 'That was Captain Young's ghost. He comes this way sometimes. Nothing to worry about, he's quite harmless. My great grandfather served under him. They say it's lucky to see his ghost.'

As I walked up the steep hill, the mist lifted and the moon came out, silvering the oaks and maples. At the old Mullingar, my white steed was waiting. A homeless ghost, like his master.

I should never have gone away. I made this place, I should have breathed my last here. And so I keep returning.

The Overcoat

It was clear, frosty weather, and as the moon came up over the Himalayan peaks, I could see that patches of snow still lay on the roads of the hill station. I would have been quite happy in bed, with a book and a hot-water bottle at my side, but I'd promised the Kapadias that I'd go to their party, and I felt it would be churlish of me to stay away. I put on two sweaters, an old football scarf and an overcoat, and set off down the moonlit road.

It was a walk of just over a mile to the Kapadias' house, and I had covered about half the distance, when I saw a girl standing in the middle of the road.

She must have been sixteen or seventeen. She looked rather old-fashioned—long hair hanging to her waist, and a flouncy sequined dress, pink and lavender, that reminded me of the photos in my grandmother's family album. When I went closer, I noticed that she had lovely eyes and a winning smile.

'Good evening,' I said. 'It's a cold night to be out.'

'Are you going to a party?' she asked.

'That's right. And I can see from your lovely dress that you're going too. Come along, we're nearly there.'

She fell into step beside me, and we soon saw lights from the Kapadias' house shining brightly through the deodars. The girl told me her name was Julie. I hadn't seen her before, but I'd only been in the hill station a few months.

There was quite a crowd at the party, and no one seemed to know Julie. Everyone thought she was friend of mine. I did not deny it. Obviously, she was someone who was feeling lonely and wanted to be friendly with people. And she was certainly enjoying herself. I did not see her do much eating or drinking, but she flitted from one group to another, talking, listening, laughing; and when the music began, she was dancing almost continuously, alone or with partners, it didn't matter which, she was completely wrapped up in music.

It was almost midnight when I got up to go. I had drunk a fair amount of punch, and I was ready for bed. As I was saying goodnight to my hosts and wishing everyone a merry Christmas, Julie slipped her arm into mine and said she'd be going home too.

When we were outside, I said, 'Where do you live, Julie?'

'At Wolfsburn,' she said. 'Right at the top of the hill.'

'There's a cold wind,' I said. 'And although your dress is beautiful, it doesn't look very warm. Here, you'd better wear my overcoat. I've plenty of protection.'

She did not protest, and allowed me to slip my overcoat over her shoulders. Then we started out on the walk home. But I did not have to escort her all the way. At about the spot where we had met, she said, 'There's a shortcut from here. I'll just scramble up the hillside.'

'Do you know it well?' I asked. 'It's a very narrow path.'

'Oh, I know every stone on the path. I use it all the time. And besides, it's a really bright night.'

'Well, keep the coat on,' I said. 'I can collect it tomorrow.'

She hesitated for a moment, then smiled and nodded. She then disappeared up the hill, and I went home alone.

The next day, I walked up to Wolfsburn. I crossed a little brook, from which the house had probably got its name, and entered an open iron gate. But of the house itself, little remained. Just a roofless ruin, a pile of stones, a shattered chimney, a few Doric pillars where a veranda had once stood.

Had Julie played a joke on me? Or had I found the wrong house?

I walked around the hill, to the mission house where the Taylors live and asked old Mrs Taylor if she knew a girl called Julie.

'No, I don't think so,' she said. 'Where does she live?'

'At Wolfsburn, I was told. But the house is just a ruin.'

'Nobody has lived at Wolfsburn for over forty years, the Mackinnons lived there. One of the old families who settled here. But when their girl died...' She stopped and gave me a queer look. 'I think her name was Julie... Anyway, when she died, they sold the house and went away. No one ever lived in it again, and it fell into decay. But it couldn't be the same Julie you're looking for. She died of consumption—there wasn't much you could do about it in those days. Her grave is in the cemetery, just down the road.'

I thanked Mrs Taylor and walked slowly down the road, to the cemetery; not really wanting to know any more, but propelled forwards almost against my will.

It was a small cemetery under the deodars. You could see the eternal snows of the Himalayas standing out against the pristine blue sky. Here lay the bones of forgotten empire-builders—soldiers, merchants, adventurers, their wives and children. It did not take me long to find Julie's grave. It had a simple headstone with her name clearly outlined on it:

Julie Mackinnon
1923–39
'*With us one moment,*
Taken the next,
Gone to her Maker,
Gone to her rest.'

And although many monsoons had swept across the cemetery, wearing down the stones, they had not touched this little tombstone.

I was turning to leave, when I got a glimpse of something familiar behind the headstone. I walked around to where it lay.

Neatly folded on the grass was my overcoat.

No thank-you note. But something soft and invisible brushed against my cheek, and I knew someone was trying to thank me.

The Black Bird

In my fortieth year, I ran into the dreaded writer's block, and seeking a change of scene, I found myself one morning in a little hamlet called Fursatganj, just outside Mussoorie. It seemed like the sort of place where nothing much happened. But three white butterflies were dancing above a raspberry bush and the Himalayas were etched against a sunny sky, so I decided to make Fursatganj my home for some months. I hoped in that time to produce at least a few stories, if not a book.

As it turned out, I did write a book many years later, calling it *Tales of Fosterganj*. It wasn't just the name of the hamlet that I changed; almost everything in that book was fiction. The truth was far stranger, and I'm revealing it here for the first time. This is how it was:

I returned to Fursatganj the next morning with my single suitcase and bedding, having rented a room the previous evening for a modest sum. The room was above a bakery run by an amiable man called Hassan, who lived a little further down the street with his family. He had fathered eleven children, he told me proudly. He called them *shaitaan ki aulaad*—spawn of the devil—for they had made him go bald and his wife prematurely grey, but he was smiling cheerfully as he said this.

In fact, everyone in Fursatganj was always smiling— the women and girls in their colourful blouses and the sarong-like ghagris popular in Garhwal, and the men and boys in kurtas and long, narrow pyjamas. They were also warning me all the time not to go out after dark or go too far into the surrounding woods. But I was a great walker in those days, and as they never told me exactly what dangers were about, I ignored their warnings.

The old bridle path from Rajpur to Mussoorie passed through Fursatganj. In the old days, before the motor road was built, this was the only road to the hill station. You could ride up on a pony, or walk, or be carried in a doolie (which was a cross between a stretcher and a sedan chair). Many years ago, a doolie, its lady occupant and two perspiring bearers had all gone over a cliff just before Fursatganj and perished in the fall. It was said that sometimes the ghost of this lady, holding a blue parasol, and the two phantom bearers could be seen on the bridle path. But they never showed themselves to me, although I spent many hours walking up and down that path hoping for a sighting.

As tales of spirits and jinns and haunted houses have always intrigued me, this was a disappointment. But soon afterwards, Hassan told me of another place to be avoided, especially after dark—the ruined palace halfway down to Rajpur. And immediately, I began to take my evening walks in its direction.

The palace was called Fairy Glen. It had been built on the lines of a Swiss chalet—a huge, rambling building with numerous turrets and balconies and cornices and windows; a wedding-cake of a palace, built to satisfy the whims and fancies of its late owner, the Raja of Ranipur, a small state near the Nepal border. Maintaining this baroque edifice must have been something of a nightmare; and the present heirs had quite given up on it, for bits of the roof were missing, some windows were without panes, doors had developed cracks, and what had once been a garden was now a small jungle. Apparently, there was no one living there anymore; no sign of a caretaker. I had walked past the wrought-iron gate several times without seeing any signs of life, apart from a large grey cat sunning itself outside a broken window.

Then one evening, walking up from Rajpur, I was caught in a storm.

A wind had sprung up, bringing with it dark, overburdened clouds. Heavy drops of rain were followed by hailstones bouncing off the stony path. Gusts of wind rushed through the oaks, and leaves and small branches were soon swirling through the air. I was still a couple of miles from the Fursatganj bazaar, and I did not fancy sheltering under a tree, as flashes of lightning were beginning to light up the darkening sky. Then I found myself at the gate of the abandoned palace.

Outside the gate stood an old sentry box. No one had stood sentry in it for years. It was a good place in which to shelter. But I hesitated because a large, strange bird was perched on the gate, silent and seemingly oblivious to the rain that was still falling.

It looked like a crow or a raven, but it was much bigger than either—and when a flash of lightning lit up the gate, it opened its great big wings and took off with a loud rustle, flying in the direction of the oak forest. I hadn't seen such a bird before; there was something dark and supernatural about it. But it had gone, and I darted into the sentry box without further delay.

1 had been standing there some ten minutes, wondering when the rain was going to stop, when I heard someone running down the road. As the apparition approached, I could see that it was a boy, probably eleven or twelve; but in the dark I could not make out his features. What was someone that young

doing in such beastly rain, and in the dark, so far away from habitation?

He came up to the gate, lifted the latch, and was about to go into the ruined palace when he saw me in the sentry box.

'Kaun? Who are you?' he asked, first in Hindi then in English. He did not appear to be in any way anxious or alarmed. And he certainly did not look like someone who had lost his way.

'Just sheltering from the rain,' I said. 'I live in the bazaar.'

He took a small torch from his pocket and shone it in my face.

'Yes, I have seen you there. A tourist.'

'No. A writer. I stay in places, I don't just pass through. And what are you doing in this wilderness?'

'What place is not a wilderness?' He surprised me by using a poetic Urdu word for it: *veeraana.* 'Do you want to come in?' he said.

I hesitated. It was still raining and the roof of the sentry box was leaking badly.

'Do you live here?' I asked.

'Yes, I am the raja's nephew. I live here with my mother. Come in.' He took me by the hand and led me through the gate. His hand was quite rough and heavy for an eleven- or twelve-year-old. Instead of walking with me to the front steps and entrance of the old palace, he led me around to the rear of the building, where a faint light glowed in a mullioned window, and in its light I saw that he had a very fresh and pleasant face—a face as yet untouched by the trials of life. But his hands... What did they know that the face did not?

Instead of knocking on the door, the boy tapped on the window. 'Only strangers knock on the door,' he said. 'When I tap on the window, my mother knows it's me.'

'That's clever of you,' I said.

He tapped again, and the door was opened by an unusually tall woman wearing a kind of loose, flowing English gown, which looked strange in that place. The light was behind her, and I couldn't see her face until we had entered the room. When she turned to me, I saw that she had a long reddish scar running down one side of her face. Even so, there was a certain hard beauty in her appearance.

'Make some tea—Mother,' said the boy rather brusquely. 'And something to eat. I'm hungry. Sir, will you have something?' He looked enquiringly at me. The light from a kerosene lamp fell full on his face. He was wide-eyed, full-lipped, smiling; only his voice seemed rather mature for one so young. And he spoke like someone much older.

'Sit down, sir.' He led me to a chair, made me comfortable. 'You are not too wet, I hope?'

'No, I took shelter before the rain came down too heavily. But you are wet, you'd better change.'

'It doesn't bother me.' And after a pause, 'Sorry, there is no electricity. Bills haven't been paid for years.'

'Is this your place?'

'No, we are only caretakers. Poor relations, you might say. The palace has been in dispute for many years. The raja and his brothers keep fighting over it, and meanwhile it is slowly falling down. The lawyers are happy. Perhaps I should study and become a lawyer some day.'

'Do you go to school?'

'Sometimes.'

'How old are you?'

'Quite old, I'm not sure. Mother, how old am I?' he asked, as the tall woman returned with cups of tea and a plate full of biscuits.

She hesitated, gave him a puzzled look. 'Don't you know?'

'I've forgotten.'

She looked at him intently, placed a hand on his shoulder, then turned to me and said, 'He is twelve.'

We finished our tea. It was still raining.

'It will rain all night,' said the boy. 'You had better stay here.'

'It will inconvenience you.'

'No, it won't. There are many rooms. If you do not mind the darkness. Come, I'll show you everything. And meanwhile my mother will make some dinner. Very simple food, I hope you won't mind.'

The boy took me around the old palace, if you could still call it that. He led the way with a candle-holder from which a large candle threw our exaggerated shadows on the walls.

'What's your name?' I asked, as he led me into what must have been a reception room, still crowded with ornate furniture and bric-a-brac.

'Bhim,' he said. 'But everyone calls me Lucky.'

'And are you lucky?'

He shrugged. 'Don't know...' Then he smiled up at me. 'Maybe you'll bring me luck.'

We walked further into the room. Large oil paintings hung from the walls, gathering mould. Some were portraits of royalty, kings and queens of another era, wearing decorative headgear, strange uniforms, the women wrapped in more jewellery than garments— and sometimes accompanied by children who were also weighed down by jewels and excessive clothing. A young man sat on a throne, his lips curled in a sardonic smile.

'My grandfather,' said Bhim.

He led me into an enormous bedroom taken up by a gigantic four-poster bed, which had probably seen several royal couples copulating upon it. It looked cold and uninviting, but Bhim produced a voluminous razai from a cupboard and assured me that it would be warm and quite luxurious, as it had been his grandfather's.

'And when did your grandfather die?' I asked.

'Oh, fifty–sixty years ago, it must have been.'

'In this bed, I suppose.'

'No, he was shot accidentally while out hunting.'

'Ah. Of course,' I said. 'What is a king who will not hunt.'

'Don't we all hunt, sir? Some more than others?'

'I suppose we do,' I said, feeling a little uncomfortable. What twelve-year-old spoke such things?

I did not feel like sleeping in that room, with its musty old draperies and paint peeling off the walls. A trickle of water from the ceiling fell down the back of my shirt and made me shiver.

'The roof is leaking,' I said. 'Maybe I'd better go home.'

'You can't go now, it's very late. And that man-eating leopard has been seen again. Surely you've heard of it?'

He fetched a china bowl from the dressing-table and placed it on the floor to catch the trickle from the ceiling. In another corner of the room a metal bucket was receiving a steady patter from another leak.

'The palace is leaking everywhere,' said Bhim. 'This is the only dry room.'

He took me by the hand and led me back to his own quarters; I was surprised, again, by how heavy and rough his hand was for a boy, and presumed that he did a certain amount of manual work such as chopping wood with a heavy axe for a daily fire. In winter the building would be unbearably cold.

His mother gave us a satisfying meal, considering the ingredients at her disposal were somewhat limited. Once again, I tried to get away. But only half-heartedly. The boy intrigued me; so did his mother; so did the rambling old palace; and the rain persisted.

Bhim the Lucky took me to my room, waited with the guttering candle till I had removed my shoes, and then handed me a pair of very large pyjamas.

'Royal pyjamas,' he said with a smile.

I got into them and floated around.

'Before you go—' I said, 'I might want to visit the bathroom in the night.'

'Of course, sir. It's close by.' He opened a door, and beyond it I saw a dark passage. 'Go a little way, and there's a door on the left. I'm leaving an extra candle and matches on the dressing table.'

He put the lighted candle he was carrying on the table, and left the room without a light. Obviously he knew his way about in the dark. His footsteps receded, and I was left alone with the sound of raindrops pattering on the roof and a loose sheet of corrugated tin roofing flapping away in a wind that had now sprung up.

It was a late spring night, and I had no need of blankets; so I removed my shoes and jacket and lay down on the capacious bed, wondering if I should blow the candle out or allow it to burn as long as it lasted.

Had I been in my own room, I would have been reading—a Conrad or a Chekhov or some other classic—because at night I turn to the classics—but here there was no light and nothing to read.

I got up and blew the candle out. I might need it later on.

Restless, I prowled around the room in the dark, banging into chairs and footstools. I made my way to the window and drew the curtains aside. Some light filtered into the room because behind the clouds there was a moon, and it had been a full moon the night before.

I lay back on the bed. It wasn't very comfortable. It was an early, outsized version of a box-bed. A royal box-bed. And although it was covered with a couple of thick mattresses, the woodwork appeared to have warped because it creaked loudly whenever I shifted my position. The boards no longer fitted properly. Either that, or the box-bed had been overstuffed with all sorts of things.

After some time I settled into one position and dozed off for a while, only to be awakened by a tapping sound somewhere, and then the sound of footsteps rushing away as I awoke and said, almost by instinct, 'Kaun?'

After a while I put my head back on the pillow and closed my eyes. But soon there was that tapping again—this time at the pane of the big French window in front of the bed. Probably the branch of a tree, swaying in the wind. But then there was a screech, and I sat up in bed. Another screech, and I was out of it.

I went to the window and pressed my face to the glass. The big black bird—the bird I had seen when taking shelter in the sentry box—was sitting, or rather squatting, on the boundary wall, facing me. The moon, now visible through the clouds, fell full upon it. Crow-like, but heavily built, like a turkey, its beak that of a bird of prey, its talons those of a vulture. I stepped back, and closed the heavy curtains, shutting out the light but also shutting out the image of that menacing bird.

Returning to the bed, I just sat there for a while, wondering if I should get up and leave. The rain had lessened. But the luminous dial of my watch showed it was two in the morning. No time for a stroll in the dark—not with a man-eating leopard in the vicinity.

Then I heard the screech again. It seemed to echo through the building. It may have been the bird, but to me it sounded all too human. There was silence for a long while after that. I lay back on the bed and tried one more time to sleep. But it was even more uncomfortable than before. Perhaps the wood had warped too much during the monsoon, I thought, and the lid of the old box-bed no longer fit properly. Maybe I could push it back into its correct position; then perhaps I could get some sleep.

So I got up again, and after fumbling around in the dark for a few minutes, found the matches and lit the tall candle, and put it on the bedside table. Then I removed the sheets from the bed and pulled away the two mattresses. The cover of the box-bed lay exposed. And a hand protruded from beneath the lid.

It was not a living hand. It was a skeletal hand, fleshless, brittle. But there was a large ring on one finger, an opal still clinging to the bone of a small index finger. It glowed faintly in the candlelight, watery-blue one instant, sharp-green the next.

Shaking a little (for I am really something of a coward, as I have said before, though an inquisitive one), I lifted the heavy lid of the box-bed, groaning with the effort. Laid out on a pretty counterpane was a skeleton. A bundle of bones, but still partly clothed in expensive-looking garments. One hand gripped the side of the box-bed; the hand that had kept it from shutting properly. As I stared, a chill going down my spine, my eyes adjusted to the dim light from the candle, and I noticed the skeleton had no feet. As if the legs had been hacked off at the shins.

That was not all. Right next to her were more skeletons. Three, perhaps four, of varying sizes, also partly clothed, but in less expensive attire. And then my hands began to tremble.

I dropped the lid of the box-bed and ran from the room—only to blunder into a locked door. Someone, presumably the boy, had locked me into the bedroom. I banged on the door and shouted, but no one heard me. No one came running. I went to the large French window, but it was firmly fastened; it probably hadn't been opened for many years.

Then I remembered the passageway leading to the bathroom. The boy had pointed it out to me. Possibly there was a way out from there. There wasn't. That door was also locked from the outside. Panic spread through me and I began to run around the room like a trapped animal. So when I heard someone say 'Huzoor!' in an urgent, loud whisper, I froze and a strangled shout escaped me.

'Huzoor! Here, quick!'

I turned around, and in a doorway at the other end of the room stood a figure wrapped in a kind of shawl or cloak, holding a lantern. In my terror and confusion I hadn't thought to check that end of the room for an exit.

But who could this be—it was a woman, I could tell that much from the whispering. What other horrors awaited me?

'You should not be here, Huzoor. There isn't much time. We must run!'

Anything to get out of there. If this was the only chance I had, I would take it.

In an instant I was at the door and following the cloaked figure. A narrow path led to a wicket-gate at the end of the building; we found our way out of the grounds. The old palace loomed out of the darkness. I turned my back on it.

My mysterious saviour was now a fair distance ahead of me, walking evenly in the night. I hurried on, and then I was back on the public road. The moon was out now, surprisingly bright, and she stopped by the side of the road.

'Never go there again, Huzoor. They have killed too many,' she said when I caught up with her. She raised a hand to wave me on and I saw an opal ring shine blue and green in the moonlight. I noticed, too, that she was floating several inches above the ground. She had no feet. And then she was a bird and she flew away into the night with a loud rustle.

I hurried on, and did not stop until I had reached my little room above Hassan's bakery.

~

I did not sleep. It was soon dawn, and when I heard Hassan open the bakery, I went down to tell him what had happened. I was still shaken.

Hassan took one look at me and he knew. 'What did you want to go there for? I told you not to,' he said.

'It was raining heavily, and I stopped near the gate to take shelter. A boy invited me in, his mother gave me something to eat…'

'That is how they lure their victims,' Hassan said.

'Victims?'

'They kill. The boy has strong hands. She holds them down and he gets to work. It is easy to strangle people when they are sleeping. That bird kept you awake. And she saved you in time. I'm not sure when she started doing that, what brought her back from the land of the dead. At least fifty had been taken by then. They would hack the legs off afterwards. The woman—she's his lover, and he's no boy, he's older than both of us. They are addicted to killing and they keep the feet as trophies.'

Hassan stopped. I think the colour had drained from my face. He waited for me to find my voice.

'How do you know all this?' I asked finally.

Hassan had been standing behind the rough wooden table where he made the dough for his breads and buns. He came over to where I was and sat on the stool next to mine. He bent down and lifted the legs of his pyjamas. His legs ended at the shins.

'When?' was all I could say.

'Twelve years ago. All of us in Fursatganj are the dead, killed by that woman and her demon lover. At some point one of us decided he did not want to cross over, and then all of us decided to stay. We loved our homes too much.'

'But I saw nothing.'

'You never looked at our feet. No one does.'

Suddenly I felt very sad and tired.

Hassan presented me with a bun and a glass of hot sweet tea while I recovered and decided what to do.

'Will you go away?' he asked. 'You don't need to. Nothing has changed. Nothing will if you don't want it to.'

Hassan was smiling. The warmth of his smile and the excellent tea and buns revived me and cleared my head. I knew what I must do. I would stay.

I spent six months in Fursatganj, and when I left, I had enough stories to make a respectable collection, and pleasant memories enough for a lifetime.

The day I left Fursatganj, I walked down to Fairy Glen one last time. It looked quite peaceful in the April sunshine. The gate was closed. There was no sign of the boy or the woman. There was no sign of the big black bird, either. Only a couple of mynas squabbling on the wall, and a black-faced langur swinging from the branch of an oak.

A *Face in the Dark*

Mr Oliver, an Anglo-Indian teacher, was returning to his school late one night, on the outskirts of the hill station of Shimla. From before Kipling's time, the school had been run on English public-school lines and the boys, most of them from wealthy Indian families, wore blazers, caps and ties. *Life* magazine, in a feature on India, had once called it the 'Eton of the East'. Mr Oliver had been teaching in the school for several years.

The Shimla Bazaar, with its cinemas and restaurants, was about three miles from the school and Mr Oliver, a bachelor, usually strolled into the town in the evening, returning after dark, when he would take a shortcut through the pine forest.

When there was a strong wind, the pine trees made sad, eerie sounds that kept most people to the main road.

But Mr Oliver was not a nervous or imaginative man. He carried a torch and its gleam—the batteries were running down—moved fitfully down the narrow forest path. When its flickering light fell on the figure of a boy who was sitting alone on a rock, Mr Oliver stopped. Boys were not supposed to be out after dark.

'What are you doing out here, boy?' asked Mr Oliver sharply, moving closer so that he could recognize the miscreant. But even as he approached the boy, Mr Oliver sensed that something was wrong. The boy appeared to be crying. His head hung down, he held his face in his hands, and his body shook convulsively. It was a strange, soundless weeping and Mr Oliver felt distinctly uneasy.

'Well, what's the matter?' he asked, his anger giving way to concern. 'What are you crying for?' The boy would not answer or look up. His body continued to be racked with silent sobbing. 'Come on, boy, you shouldn't be out here at this hour. Tell me the trouble. Look up!' The boy looked up. He took his hands from his face and looked up at his teacher. The light from Mr Oliver's torch fell on the boy's face—if you could call it a face.

It had no eyes, ears, nose or mouth. It was just a round smooth head—with a school cap on top of it! And that's where the story should end. But for Mr Oliver it did not end here.

The torch fell from his trembling hand. He turned and scrambled down the path, running blindly through the trees and calling for help. He was still running towards the school buildings when he saw a lantern swinging in the middle of the path. Mr Oliver stumbled up to the watchman, gasping for breath. 'What is it, sahib?' asked the watchman. 'Has there been an accident? Why are you running?'

'I saw something—something horrible—a boy weeping in the forest—and he had no face!'

'No face, sahib?'

'No eyes, nose, mouth—nothing!'

'Do you mean it was like this, sahib?' asked the watchman and raised the lamp to his own face. The watchman had no eyes, no ears, no features at all—not even an eyebrow! And that's when the wind blew the lamp out.

Wilson's Bridge

The old wooden bridge has gone, and today an iron suspension bridge straddles the Bhagirathi as it rushes down the gorge below Gangotri. But villagers will tell you that you can still hear the hoofs of Wilson's horse as he gallops across the bridge he had built a hundred and fifty years ago. At the time people were sceptical of its safety, and so to prove its sturdiness, he rode across it again and again. Parts of the old bridge can still be seen on the far bank of the river. And the legend of Wilson and his pretty hill bride, Gulabi, is still well known in this region.

I had joined some friends in the old forest rest house near the river. There were the Rays, recently married, and the Dattas, married many years. The younger Rays quarrelled frequently; the older Dattas looked on with more amusement than concern. I was a part of their group and yet something of an outsider. As a single man, I was a person of no importance. And as a marriage counsellor, I wouldn't have been of any use to them.

I spent most of my time wandering along the river banks or exploring the thick deodar and oak forests that covered the slopes. It was these trees that had made a fortune for Wilson and his patron, the Raja of Tehri. They had exploited the great forests to the full, floating huge logs downstream to the timber yards in the plains.

Returning to the rest house late one evening, I was halfway across the bridge when I saw a figure at the other end, emerging from the mist. Presently I made out a woman, wearing the plain dhoti of the hills; her hair fell loose over her shoulders. She appeared not to see me, and reclined against the railing of the bridge, looking down at the rushing waters far below. And then, to my amazement and horror, she climbed over the railing and threw herself into the river.

I ran forward, calling out, but I reached the railing only to see her fall into the foaming waters below, where she was carried swiftly downstream.

The watchman's cabin stood a little way off. The door was open. The watchman, Ram Singh, was reclining on his bed, smoking a hookah.

'Someone just jumped off the bridge,' I said breathlessly. 'She's been swept down the river!'

The watchman was unperturbed. 'Gulabi again,' he said, almost to himself; and then to me, 'Did you see her clearly?'

'Yes, a woman with long loose hair—but I didn't see her face very clearly.'

'It must have been Gulabi, only a ghost, my dear sir. Nothing to be alarmed about. Every now and then someone sees her throw herself into the river. Sit down,' he said, gesturing towards a battered old armchair, 'be comfortable and I'll tell you all about it.'

I was far from comfortable, but I listened to Ram Singh tell me the tale of Gulabi's suicide. After making me a glass of hot sweet tea, he launched into a long rambling account of how Wilson, a British adventurer seeking his fortune, had been hunting musk deer when he encountered Gulabi on the path from her village. The girl's grey-green eyes and peach-blossom complexion enchanted him, and he went out of his way to get to know her people. Was he in love with her or did he simply find her beautiful and desirable? We shall never really know. In the course of his travels and adventures he had known many women, but Gulabi was different, childlike and ingenuous, and he decided he would marry her. The humble family to which she belonged had no objection. Hunting had its limitations, and Wilson found it more profitable to trap the region's great forest wealth. In a few years he had made a fortune. He built a large timbered house at Harsil, another in Dehradun, and a third at Mussoorie. Gulabi had all she could have wanted, including two robust little sons. When he was away on work, she looked after their children and their large apple orchard at Harsil.

And then came the evil day when Wilson met the Englishwoman, Ruth, on the Mussoorie mall, and decided that she should have a share of his affections and his wealth. A fine house was provided for her too. The time he spent at Harsil with Gulabi and his children dwindled. 'Business affairs'—he was now one of the owners of a bank—kept him in the fashionable hill resort. He was a popular host and took his friends and associates on shikar parties in the Boon.

Gulabi brought up her children in village style. She heard stories of Wilson's dalliance with the Mussoorie woman and, on one of his rare visits, she confronted him and voiced her resentment, demanding that he leave the other woman. He brushed her aside and told her not to listen to idle gossip. When he turned away from her, she picked up the flintlock pistol that lay on the gun table, and fired one shot at him. The bullet missed him and shattered her looking-glass. Gulabi ran out of the house, through the orchard and into the forest, then down the steep path to the bridge built by

Wilson only two or three years before. When he had recovered his composure, he mounted his horse and came looking for her. It was too late. She had already thrown herself off the bridge into the swirling waters far below. Her body was found a mile or two downstream, caught between some rocks.

This was the tale that Ram Singh told me, with various flourishes and interpolations of his own. I thought it would make a good story to tell my friends that evening, before the fireside in the rest house. They found the story fascinating, but when I told them I had seen Gulabi's ghost, they thought I was doing a little embroidering of my own. Mrs Dutta thought it was a tragic tale. Young Mrs Ray thought Gulabi had been very silly. 'She was a simple girl,' opined Mr Dutta. 'She responded in the only way she knew…' 'Money can't buy happiness,' said Mr Ray. 'No,' said Mrs Dutta, 'but it can buy you a great many comforts.' Mrs Ray wanted to talk of other things, so I changed the subject. It can get a little confusing for a bachelor who must spend the evening with two married couples. There are undercurrents which he is aware of but not equipped to deal with.

I would walk across the bridge quite often after that. It was busy with traffic during the day, but after dusk there were only a few vehicles on the road and seldom any pedestrians. A mist rose from the gorge below and obscured the far end of the bridge. I preferred walking there in the evening, half-expecting, half-hoping to see Gulabi's ghost again. It was her face that I really wanted to see. Would she still be as beautiful as she was fabled to be?

It was on the evening before our departure that something happened that would haunt me for a long time afterwards.

There was a feeling of restiveness as our days there drew to a close. The Rays had apparently made up their differences, although they weren't talking very much. Mr Dutta was anxious to get back to his office in Delhi and Mrs Dutta's rheumatism was playing up. I was restless, too, wanting to return to my writing desk in Mussoorie.

That evening I decided to take one last stroll across the bridge to enjoy the cool breeze of a summer's night in the mountains. The moon hadn't come up, and it was really quite dark, although there were lamps at either end of the bridge providing sufficient light for those who wished to cross over.

I was standing in the middle of the bridge, in the darkest part, listening to the river thundering down the gorge, when I saw the sari-draped figure emerging from the lamplight and making towards the railings.

Instinctively I called out, 'Gulabi!'

She half-turned towards me, but I could not see her clearly. The wind had blown her hair across her face and all I saw was wildly staring eyes. She raised herself over the railing and threw herself off the bridge. I heard the splash as her body struck the water far below.

Once again I found myself running towards the part of the railing where she had jumped. And then someone was running towards the same spot, from the direction of the rest house. It was young Mr Ray.

'My wife!' he cried out. 'Did you see my wife?'

He rushed to the railing and stared down at the swirling waters of the river.

'Look! There she is!' He pointed at a helpless figure bobbing about in the water.

We ran down the steep bank to the river but the current had swept her on. Scrambling over rocks and bushes, we made frantic efforts to catch up with the drowning woman. But the river in that defile is a roaring torrent, and it was over an hour before we were able to retrieve poor Mrs Ray's body, caught in driftwood about a mile downstream.

She was cremated not far from where we found her and we returned to our various homes in gloom and grief, chastened but none the wiser for the experience.

If you happen to be in that area and decide to cross the bridge late in the evening, you might see Gulabi's ghost or hear the hoof-beats of Wilson's horse as he canters across the old wooden bridge looking for her.

Or you might see the ghost of Mrs Ray and hear her husband's anguished cry. Or there might be others. Who knows?

The Whistler

The moon was almost at the full. Bright moonlight flooded the road. But I was stalked by the shadows of the trees, by the crooked oak branches reaching out towards me—some threateningly, others as though they needed companionship.

Once, I dreamt that the trees could walk. That on moonlit nights like this they would uproot themselves for a while, visit each other, talk about old times—for they had seen many men and happenings, especially the older ones. And then, before dawn, they would return to the places where they had been condemned to grow. Lonely sentinels of the night. And this was a good night for them to walk. They appeared eager to do so: a restless rustling of leaves, the creaking of branches—these were sounds that came from within them in the silence of the night...

Occasionally other strollers passed me in the dark. It was still quite early, just eight o'clock, and some people were on their way home. Others were walking into town for a taste of the bright lights, shops and restaurants. On the unlit road I could not recognize them. They did not notice me. I was reminded of an old song from my childhood. Softly, I began humming the tune, and soon the words came back to me:

> *We three,*
> *We're not a crowd;*
> *We're not even company—*
> *My echo,*
> *My shadow,*
> *And me...*

I looked down at my shadow, moving silently beside me. We take our shadows for granted, don't we? There they are, the uncomplaining companions of a lifetime, mute and helpless witnesses to our every act of commission or omission. On this bright moonlit night I could not help noticing you, Shadow, and I was sorry that you had to see so much that I was ashamed of; but glad, too, that you were around when I had my small triumphs. And what of my echo? I thought of calling out to see if my call came back to me; but I refrained from doing so, as I did not wish to disturb the perfect stillness of the mountains or the conversations of the trees.

The road wound up the hill and levelled out at the top, where it became a ribbon of moonlight entwined between tall deodars. A flying squirrel glided across the road, leaving one tree for another. A nightjar called. The rest was silence.

The old cemetery loomed up before me. There were many old graves—some large and monumental—and there were a few recent graves too, for the cemetery was still in use. I could see flowers scattered on one of them—a few late dahlias and scarlet salvia. Further on, near the boundary wall, part of the cemetery's retaining wall had collapsed in the heavy monsoon rains. Some of the tombstones had come down with the wall. One grave lay exposed. A rotting coffin and a few scattered bones were the only relics of someone who had lived and loved like you and me.

Part of the tombstone lay beside the road, but the lettering had worn away. I am not normally a morbid person, but something made me stoop and pick up a smooth round shard of bone, probably part of a skull. When my hand closed over it, the bone crumbled into fragments. I let them fall to the grass. Dust to dust.

And from somewhere, not too far away, came the sound of someone whistling.

At first I thought it was another late-evening stroller, whistling to himself much as I had been humming my old song. But the whistler approached quite rapidly; the whistling was loud and cheerful. A boy on a bicycle sped past. I had only a glimpse of him, before his cycle went weaving through the shadows on the road.

But he was back again in a few minutes. And this time he stopped a few feet away from me, and gave me a quizzical half-smile. A slim dusky boy of fourteen or fifteen. He wore a school blazer and a yellow scarf. His eyes were pools of liquid moonlight.

'You don't have a bell on your cycle,' I said.

He said nothing, just smiled at me with his head a little to one side. I put out my hand, and I thought he was going to take it. But then, quite suddenly, he was off again, whistling cheerfully though rather tunelessly. A whistling schoolboy. A bit late for him to be out, but he seemed an independent sort.

The whistling grew fainter, then faded away altogether. A deep sound-denying silence fell upon the forest. My shadow and I walked home.

Next morning I woke to a different kind of whistling— the song of the thrush outside my window.

It was a wonderful day, the sunshine warm and sensuous, and I longed to be out in the open. But there was work to be done, proofs to be corrected, letters to be written. And it was several days before I could walk to the top of the hill, to that lonely tranquil resting place under the deodars. It seemed to me ironic that those who had the best view of the glistening snow-capped peaks were all buried several feet underground.

Some repair work was going on. The retaining wall of the cemetery was being shored up, but the overseer told me that there was no money to restore the damaged grave. With the help of the chowkidar, I returned the scattered bones to a little hollow under the collapsed masonry, and I left some money with him so that he could have the open grave bricked up. The name on the gravestone had worn away, but I could make out a date—20 November 1950—some fifty years ago, but not too long ago as gravestones go…

I found the burial register in the church vestry and turned back the yellowing pages to 1950, when I was just a schoolboy myself. I found the name there—Michael Dutta, aged fifteen—and the cause of death: road accident.

Well, I could only make guesses. And to turn conjecture into certainty, I would have to find an old resident who might remember the boy or the accident.

There was old Miss Marley at Pine Top. A retired teacher from Woodstock, she had a wonderful memory, and she had lived in the hill station for more than half a century.

White-haired and smooth-cheeked, her bright blue

eyes full of curiosity, she gazed benignly at me through her old-fashioned pince-nez.

'Michael was a charming boy—full of exuberance, always ready to oblige. I had only to mention that I needed a newspaper or an Aspirin, and he'd be off on his bicycle, swooping down these steep roads with great abandon. But these hill roads, with their sudden corners, weren't meant for racing around on a bicycle. They were widening our road for motor traffic, and a truck was coming uphill, loaded with rubble, when Michael came round a bend and smashed headlong into it. He was rushed to the hospital, and the doctors did their best, but he did not recover consciousness. Of course you must have seen his grave. That's why you're here. His parents? They left shortly afterwards. Went abroad, I think… A charming boy, Michael, but just a bit too reckless. You'd have liked him, I think.'

I did not see the phantom bicycle-rider again for some time, although I felt his presence on more than one occasion. And when on a cold winter's evening, I walked past that lonely cemetery, I thought I heard him whistling far away. But he did not manifest himself. Perhaps it was only the echo of a whistle, in communion with my insubstantial shadow.

It was several months before I saw that smiling face again. And then it came at me out of the mist as I was walking home in drenching monsoon rain. I had been to a dinner party at the old community centre, and I was returning home along a very narrow, precipitous path known as the Eyebrow. A storm had been threatening all evening. A heavy mist had settled on the hillside. It was so thick that the light from my torch simply bounced off it. The sky blossomed with sheet lightning and thunder rolled over the mountains. The rain became heavier. I moved forward slowly, carefully, hugging the hillside. There was a clap of thunder, and then I saw him emerge from the mist and stand in my way—the same slim dark youth who had materialized near the cemetery. He did not smile. Instead he put up his hand and waved me back. I hesitated, stood still. The mist lifted a little, and I saw that the path had disappeared. There was a gaping emptiness a few feet in front of me. And then a drop of over a hundred feet to the rocks below.

As I stepped back, clinging to a thorn bush for support, the boy vanished. I stumbled back to the community centre and spent the night on a chair in the library.

I did not see him again.

But weeks later, when I was down with a severe bout of flu, I heard him from my sickbed, whistling beneath my window. Was he calling to me to join him, I wondered, or was he just trying to reassure me that all was well? I got out of bed and looked out, but I saw no one. From time to time I heard his whistling; but as I got better, it grew fainter until it ceased altogether.

Fully recovered, I renewed my old walks to the top of the hill. But although I lingered near the cemetery until it grew dark, and paced up and down the deserted road, I did not see or hear the whistler again. I felt lonely, in need of a friend, even if it was only a phantom bicycle-rider. But there were only the trees.

And so every evening I walk home in the darkness, singing the old refrain:

> *We three,*
> *We're not alone,*
> *We're not even company—*
> *My echo,*
> *My shadow,*
> *And me…*

The Ghost in the Garden

Behind the house there was an orchard where guava, lichee and papaya trees mingled with two or three tall mango trees. The guava trees were easy to climb. The lichee trees gave lot of shade—as well as bunches of delicious lichees in the summer. The mango trees were at their most attractive in the spring, when their blossoms gave out a heady fragrance.

But there was one old mango tree, near the boundary wall, where no one, not even Dhuki the gardener, ever went.

'It doesn't give any fruit,' said Dhuki, when I questioned him. 'It's an old tree.'

'Then why don't we cut it down?'

'We will, one day, when your grandmother wishes…'

The weeds grew thick in that corner of the garden. They were safe there from Dhuki's relentless weeding.

'Why doesn't anyone go to that corner of the orchard?' I asked Miss Kellner, our crippled tenant, who had been in Dehra since she was a girl.

But she didn't want to talk about it. Uncle Ken, too, changed the subject whenever I brought it up.

So I wandered about the orchard on my own, cautiously making my way towards that neglected and forbidden corner of the garden until Dhuki called me back.

'Don't go there, baba,' he cautioned. 'It's unlucky.'

'Why doesn't anyone go near the old mango tree?' I asked Granny.

She just shook her head and turned away. There was obviously something that no one wanted me to know. So I disobeyed and ignored everyone, and in the still of the afternoon, when most of the household was taking a siesta, I walked over to the old mango tree at the end of the garden.

It was a cool, shady place, and seemed friendly enough. But there were no birds in the tree; no squirrels, either. And this was unusual. I sat down on the grass, with my back against the trunk of the tree, and peered out at the sunlit house and garden. In the shimmering heat haze I thought I saw someone walking through the trees, but it wasn't Dhuki or anyone I knew.

It had been a hot day, but presently I began to feel cold; and then I found myself shivering, as though a fever had suddenly come on. I looked up into the tree, and the branch above me was moving, swaying slightly, although there was no breeze and all the other leaves and branches were still.

I felt I had to get out of the cold, but I found it difficult to get up. So I crawled across the grass on my hands and knees, until I was in the bright sunlight. The shivering passed and I ran across to the house and did not look back at the mango tree until I had reached the verandah.

I told Miss Kellner about my experience.

'Were you frightened?' she asked.

'Yes—a little,' I confessed.

'And did you see anything?'

'Some of the branches moved—I felt very cold—but there was no wind.'

'Did you hear anything?'

'Just a soft moaning sound.'

'It's an old tree. It groans when it feels its age—just as I do!'

I did not go near the mango tree for some time, and I did not mention the incident to Granny or Uncle Ken. I had by now realized that the subject was taboo with them.

~

As a boy I was always exploring lonely places—neglected gardens and orchards, unoccupied houses, patches of scrub or wasteland, the fields outside the town, the fringes of the forest. On one of my rambles behind the bungalow, I pushed my way through a thicket of lantana bushes and stumbled over a thick stone slab, twisting my ankle slightly as I fell. For some time I sat on the grass, massaging my foot. When the pain eased, I looked more closely at the stone slab and was surprised to find that it was a gravestone. It was almost entirely covered by ivy; obviously no one had been near it for years. I tugged at the ivy and some of it came away in my hands. There was some indistinct lettering on the grave, half-obscured by grass and moss. I could make out a name—Rose—but little more.

I sat there for some time, pondering over my discovery, and wondering why 'Rose' should have been buried at so lonely a spot when there was a cemetery not far away. Why hadn't she been interred beside her kith and kin? Had she wished it so? And why?

Only Miss Kellner seemed willing to answer my questions, and it was to her I went, where she sat in her armchair under the pomalo tree—the armchair from which she never moved except when she was carried bodily to her bed or bathroom by the ayah or a couple of her rickshaw boys. I can never forget crippled Miss Kellner in her armchair in the garden, playing patience with a well-worn pack of cards—and always patient with me whenever I interrupted her game with endless questions about neighbours or relatives or her own history. Even as a boy, the past fascinated me. I don't mean the history of nations; I mean individual histories, the way people lived, and why they were happy or unhappy, and why they sometimes did terrible things for no apparent rhyme or reason.

'Miss Kellner,' I asked, 'whose grave is that in the jungle behind the house?'

She looked at me over the rim of her pince-nez. 'How would you expect me to know, child? Do I look as though I could climb walls, looking for old graves? Have you asked your grandmother?'

'Granny won't tell me anything. And Uncle Ken pretends to know everything when he knows nothing.'

'You've been here a long time'.

'Only twenty years. That happened before I came to this house.'

'What happened?'

'Oh, you are a trying boy. Why must you know everything?'

'It's better than not knowing.'

'Are you sure? Sometimes it's better not to know.'

'Sometimes, maybe… But I like to know. Who was Rose?'

'Your grandfather's first wife.'

'Oh.' This came as a surprise. I hadn't heard about grandfather's first marriage. 'But why is she buried in such a lonely place? Why not in the cemetery?'

'Because she took her own life. And in those days suicide couldn't be given Christian burial in a cemetery. Now is your curiosity satisfied?'

But my appetite had only been whetted for more information. 'And why did she commit suicide?'

'I really don't know, child. Why would anyone? Because they are unhappy, tired of living, in distress over something or the other.'

'You're not tired of living, are you? Even though you can't walk and your fingers are all crooked…'

'Don't be rude, or you won't find any meringues in my pantry! My fingers are good enough for writing, and for poking small boys in the ribs.' And she gave me a sharp poke which made me yelp. 'No, I'm not tired of life—not yet—but people are made differently, you know. And your grandfather isn't around to tell us what happened. And of course he married again—your grandmother.'

'Would she have known the first one?'

'I don't think so. She met your grandfather much later. But she doesn't like to talk about these things.'

'And how did Rose commit suicide?'

'I have no idea.'

'Of course you know, Miss Kellner. You can't bluff me. You know everything!'

'I wasn't there, I tell you.'

'But you heard all about it. And I know how she did it. She must have hanged herself from that mango tree—the tree at the end of the garden, which everyone avoids. I told you I went there one day, and it was very cold and lonely in its shade. I was frightened, you know.'

'Yes,' said Miss Kellner pensively. 'She must have been lonely, poor thing. She wasn't very stable, I'm told. Used to wander about on her own, picking wildflowers, singing to herself, sometimes getting lost and coming home at odd hours. How does the old song go? Lonely as the desert breeze…' In her croaky voice, Miss Kellner sang a refrain from an old ballad, before continuing, 'Your grandfather was very fond of her. He wasn't a cruel man. He put up with her strange ways. But sometimes he lost patience and scolded her and once or twice had even to lock her up. That was frightening, because then she would start screaming. It was a mistake—locking her up. Never lock anyone up, child… Something seemed to snap inside her. She became violent at times.'

'How do you know all this, Miss Kellner?'

'Your grandfather would sometimes come over and tell me his troubles. I was living in another house then, a little way down the road. Poor man, he had a trying time with Rose. He was thinking of sending her to Ranchi, to the mental hospital. Then, early one morning, he found her hanging from the mango tree. Her spirit had flown away, like the bluebird she always wanted to be.'

~

After that, I did not go near the old mango tree; I found it rather menacing, as though it had actually participated in the dark deed… Poor innocent tree, being saddled with the emotions of unbalanced humans! But I did visit the neglected grave and cleaned the weeds away, so that the inscription came out more clearly 'Rose, dearly beloved wife of Henry—(my maternal grandfather's surname followed). And when Dhuki wasn't looking, I plucked a red rose from the garden and placed it on the grave.

One afternoon, when Granny was at a bridge-party and Uncle Ken was taking a walk, I rummaged through the old storeroom adjoining the back veranda, leafing through old scrapbook and magazines. Behind a pile of books I discovered an old wind-up gramophone, an album of well-preserved gramophone records, and box of steel needles. I took the gramophone into the sitting-room and tried out one of the records. It sounded all right. So I played a few more. They were all songs of yesteryear, romantic ballads sung by tenors and baritones who were popular in the 1920s and '30s. Granny did not listen to music, and the gramophone had been neglected a long time. Now, for the first time in many years, the room was full of melody. One alone, I'll see you again, Will you remember? Only a rose…

> *Only a rose*
> *To give you,*
> *Only a song*
> *Dying away,*
> *Only a smile*
> *To keep in memory.*

It was while this tender love song was playing that a transformation seemed to come over the room.

At first it grew darker. Then a soft pink glow suffused the room, and I saw the figure of a woman, a smiling melancholy woman in white, drifting, rather than walking, towards me. She stopped in the centre of the room, and appeared to be watching me. She wore the long, flowing dress of an earlier day, and her hair was arranged in a sort of coiffure that I'd seen in old photographs.

As the song came to an end, the apparition vanished. The room was normal again. I put away the gramophone and the records. I felt disturbed rather than afraid, and I did not wish to conjure up further emanations from the past.

But in my dreams that night I saw the beautiful sad lady again. She was waltzing in the garden, sometimes by herself, sometimes partnered by other phantom dancers. She beckoned to me in my dreams, inviting me to join her, but I remained standing on the veranda steps until she danced away into the distance and faded from view.

And in the morning when I woke I found a red rose, moist with dew, lying beside my pillow.

The Haunted Bicycle

I was living at the time in a village in the foothills about five miles from a town called Shahganj, and my only means of transport was a bicycle. I could of course have gone into Shahganj on any obliging farmer's bullock-cart, but, in spite of bad roads and my own clumsiness as a cyclist, I found the bicycle a trifle faster. I went down to Shahganj almost every day, collected my mail, bought a newspaper, drank innumerable cups of tea, and gossiped with the tradesmen. I cycled back to the village at about six in the evening along a quiet, unfrequented forest road. During the winter months it was dark by six, and I would have to use a lamp on the bicycle.

One evening, when I had covered about half the distance to the village, I was brought to a halt by a small boy who was standing in the middle of the road. The forest at that late hour was no place for a child: wolves and hyenas were common in the district. I got down from my bicycle and approached the boy, but he didn't seem to take much notice of me.

'What are you doing here on your own?' I asked.

'I'm waiting,' he said, without looking at me.

'Waiting for whom? Your parents?'

'No, I am waiting for my sister.'

'Well, I haven't passed her on the road,' I said. 'She may be further ahead. You had better come along with me, we'll soon find her.'

The boy nodded and climbed silently on to the crossbar in front of me. I have never been able to recall his features. Already it was dark and besides, he kept his face turned away from me.

The wind was against us, and as I cycled on, I shivered with the cold, but the boy did not seem to feel it. We had not gone far when the light from my lamp fell on the figure of another child who was standing by the side of the road. This time it was a girl. She was a little older than the boy, and her hair was long and windswept, hiding most of her face.

'Here's your sister,' I said. 'Let's take her along with us.'

The girl did not respond to my smile, and she did no more than nod seriously to the boy. But she climbed up on to my back carrier, and allowed me to pedal off again. Their replies to my friendly questions were monosyllabic, and I gathered that they were wary of strangers. Well, when I got to the village, I would hand them over to the headman, and he could locate their parents.

The road was level, but I felt as though I was cycling uphill. And then I noticed that the boy's head was much closer to my face, that the girl's breathing was loud and heavy, almost as though she was doing the riding. Despite the cold wind, I began to feel hot and suffocated.

'I think we'd better take a rest,' I suggested.

'No!' cried the boy and girl together. 'No rest!'

I was so surprised that I rode on without any argument; and then, just as I was thinking of ignoring their demand and stopping, I noticed that the boy's hands, which were resting on the handlebar, had grown long and black and hairy.

My hands shook and the bicycle wobbled about on the road.

'Be careful!' shouted the children in unison. 'Look where you're going!'

Their tone now was menacing and far from childlike. I took a quick glance over my shoulder and had my worst fears confirmed. The girl's face was huge and bloated. Her legs, black and hairy, were trailing along the ground.

'Stop!' ordered the terrible children. 'Stop near the stream!'

But before I could do anything, my front wheel hit a stone and the bicycle toppled over. As I sprawled in the dust, I felt something hard, like a hoof, hit me on the back of the head, and then there was total darkness.

When I recovered consciousness, I noticed that the moon had risen and was sparkling on the waters of a stream. The children were not to be seen anywhere. I got up from the ground and began to brush the dust from my clothes. And then, hearing the sound of splashing and churning in the stream, I looked up again.

Two small black buffaloes gazed at me from the muddy, moonlit water.

Binya

While I was walking home one day, along the path through the pines, I heard a girl singing.

It was summer in the hills, and the trees were in new leaf. The walnuts and cherries were just beginning to form between the leaves

The wind was still and the trees were hushed, and the song came to me clearly; but it was not the words—which I could not follow—or the rise and fall of the melody which held me in thrall, but the voice itself, which was a young and tender voice.

I left the path and scrambled down the slope, slipping on fallen pine needles. But when I came to the bottom of the slope, the singing had stopped and there was no one there. 'I'm sure I heard someone singing,' I said to myself and then thought I might have been wrong. In the hills it is always possible to be wrong.

So I walked on home, and presently I heard another song, but this time it was the whistling thrush rendering a broken melody, singing a dark, sweet secret in the depths of the forest.

I had little to sing about myself. The electricity bill hadn't been paid, and there was nothing in the bank, and my second novel had just been turned down by another publisher. Still, it was summer and men and animals were drowsy, and so were my creditors. The distant mountains loomed purple in the shimmering dust haze.

I walked through the pines again, but I did not hear the singing. And then for a week I did not leave the cottage, as the novel had to be rewritten, and I worked hard at it, pausing only to eat and sleep and take note of the leaves turning a darker green.

The window opened on to the forest. Trees reached up to the window. Oak, maple, walnut. Higher up the hill, the pines started and further on, armies of deodars marched over the mountains. And the mountains rose higher, and the trees grew stunted until they finally disappeared and only the black spirit-haunted rocks rose up to meet the everlasting snows. Those peaks cradled the sky. I could not see them from my windows. But on clear mornings they could be seen from the pass on the Tehri road.

There was a stream at the bottom of the hill. One morning, quite early, I went down to the stream, and using the boulders as stepping stones, moved downstream for about half a mile. Then I lay down to rest on a flat rock in the shade of a wild cherry tree and watched the sun shifting through the branches as it rose over the hill called Pari Tibba (Fairy Hill) and slid down the steep slope into the valley. The air was very still and already the birds were silent. The only sound came from the water running over the stony bed of the stream. I had lain there ten, perhaps fifteen, minutes when I began to feel that someone was watching me.

Someone in the trees, in the shadows, still and watchful. Nothing moved; not a stone shifted, not a twig broke. But someone was watching me. I felt terribly exposed; not to danger, but to the scrutiny of unknown eyes. So I left the rock and, finding a path through the trees, began climbing the hill again.

It was warm work. The sun was up, and there was no breeze. I was perspiring profusely by the time I got to the top of the hill. There was no sign of my unseen watcher. Two lean cows grazed on the short grass; the tinkling of their bells was the only sound in the sultry summer air.

That song again! The same song, the same singer. I heard her from my window. And putting aside the book I was reading, I leant out of the window and started down through the trees. But the foliage was too heavy and the singer too far away for me to be able to make her out. 'Should I go and look for her?' I wondered. 'Or is it better this way—heard but not seen? For, having fallen in love with a song, must it follow that I will fall in love with the singer? No. But surely it is the voice and not the song that has touched me…' Presently the singing ended, and I turned away from the window.

A girl was gathering bilberries on the hillside. She was fresh-faced, honey-coloured. Her lips were stained with purple juice. She smiled at me. 'Are they good to eat?' I asked.

She opened her fist and thrust out her hand, which was full of berries, bruised and crushed. I took one and put it in my mouth. It had a sharp, sour taste. 'It is good,' I said. Finding that I could speak haltingly in her language, she came nearer, said, 'Take more then,' and filled my hand with bilberries. Her fingers touched mine. The sensation was almost unique, for it was nine or ten years since my hand had touched a girl's.

'Where do you live?' I asked. She pointed across the valley to where a small village straddled the slopes of a terraced hill.

'It's quite far,' I said. 'Do you always come so far from home?'

'I go further than this,' she said. 'The cows must find fresh grass. And there is wood to gather and grass to cut.'

She showed me the sickle held by the cloth tied firmly about her waist. 'Sometimes I go to the top of Pari Tibba, sometimes to the valley beyond. Have you been there?'

'No. But I will go some day.'

'It is always windy on Pari Tibba.'

'Is it true that there are fairies there?'

She laughed. 'That is what people say. But those are people who have never been there. I do not see fairies on Pari Tibba. It is said there are ghosts in the ruins on the hill. But I do not see any ghosts.'

'I have heard of the ghosts,' I said. 'Two lovers who ran away and took shelter in a ruined cottage. At night there was a storm, and they were killed by lightning. Is it true, this story?'

'It happened many years ago, before I was born. I have heard the story. But there are no ghosts on Pari Tibba.'

'How old are you?' I asked.

'Fifteen, sixteen, I do not know for sure.'

'Doesn't your mother know?'

'She is dead. And my grandmother has forgotten. And my brother, he is younger than me and he's forgotten his own age. Is it important to remember?'

'No, it is not important. Not here, anyway. Not in the hills. To a mountain, a hundred years are but as a day.'

'Are you very old?' she asked.

'I hope not. Do I look very old?'

'Only a hundred,' she said, and laughed, and the silver

bangles on her wrists tinkled as she put her hands up to her laughing face.

'Why do you laugh?' I asked.

'Because you looked as though you believed me. How old are you?'

'Thirty-five, thirty-six, I do not remember.'

'Ah, it is better to forget!'

'That's true,' I said, 'but sometimes one has to fill in forms and things like that, and then one has to state one's age.'

'I have never filled a form. I have never seen one.'

'And I hope you never will. It is a piece of paper covered with useless information. It is all a part of human progress.'

'Progress?'

'Yes. Are you unhappy?'

'No.'

'Do you go hungry?'

'No.'

'Then you don't need progress. Wild bilberries are better.'

She went away without saying goodbye. The cows had strayed and she ran after them, calling them by name: 'Neelu, Neelu!' and 'Bhuri!' Her bare feet moved swiftly over the rocks and dry grass.

~

Early May. The cicadas were singing in the forest; or rather, orchestrating, since they make the sound with their legs. The whistling thrushes pursued each other over the treetops in acrobatic love flights. Sometimes the langoors visited the oak trees to feed on the leaves. As I moved down the path to the stream, I heard the same singing, and coming suddenly upon the clearing near the water's edge I saw the girl sitting on a rock, her feet in the rushing water—the same girl who had given me bilberries. Strangely enough, I had not guessed that she was the singer. Unseen voices conjure up fanciful images. I had imagined a woodland nymph, a graceful, delicate, beautiful, goddess-like creature, not a mischievous-eyed, round-faced, juice-stained, slightly ragged pixie. Her dhoti—a rough, homespun sari—was faded and torn; an impractical garment, I thought, for running about on the hillside, but the village folk put their girls into dhotis before they are twelve. She'd compromised by hitching it up and by strengthening the waist with a length of cloth bound tightly about her, but she'd have been more at ease in the long, flounced skirt worn in the hills further away.

But I was not disillusioned. I had clearly taken a fancy to her cherubic, open countenance; and the sweetness of her voice added to her charms.

I watched her from the banks of the stream, and

presently she looked up, grinned, and stuck her tongue
out at me.

'That's a nice way to greet me,' I said. 'Have I offended
you?'

'You surprised me. Why did you not call out?'

'Because I was listening to your singing. I did not
wish to speak until you had finished.'

'It was only a song.'

'But you sang it sweetly.'

She smiled. 'Have you brought anything to eat?'

'No. Are you hungry?'

'At this time I get hungry. When you come to meet
me you must always bring something to eat.'

'But I didn't come to meet you. I didn't know you
would be here.'

'You do not wish to meet me?'

'I didn't mean that. It is nice to meet you.'

'You will meet me if you keep coming into the forest.
So always bring something to eat.'

'I will do so next time. Shall I pick you some berries?'

'You will have to go to the top of the hill again to find
the kingora bushes.'

'I don't mind. If you are hungry, I will bring some.'

'All right,' she said, and looked down at her feet, which
were still in the water.

Like some knight-errant of old, I toiled up the hill

again until I found the bilberry bushes, and stuffing my pockets with berries I returned to the stream. But when I got there I found she'd slipped away. The cowbells tinkled on the far hill.

The sun went down and behind the mountains as I walked home. Glow-worms shone fitfully in the dark. The night was full of sounds—the tonk-tonk of a nightjar, the cry of a barking deer, the shuffling of porcupines, the soft flip-fop of moths beating against the windowpanes. On the hill across the valley, lights flickered in the small village—the dim lights of kerosene lamps swinging in the dark.

'What is your name?' I asked, when we met again on the path through the pine forest.

'Binya,' she said. 'What is yours?'

'I have no name.'

'All right, Mr No-name.'

'I mean I haven't made a name for myself. We must make our own names, don't you think?'

'Binya is my name. I do not wish to have any other. Where are you going?'

'Nowhere.'

'No-name goes nowhere! Then you cannot come with me, because I am going home and my grandmother will set the village dogs on you if you follow me.' And laughing, she ran down the path to the stream; she knew I could not catch up with her.

One day, it was raining when I saw her. Her face streamed summer rain as she climbed the steep hill, calling the white cow home. She seemed very tiny on the windswept mountainside. A twist of hair lay flat against her forehead and her torn blue dhoti clung to her firm round thighs. I went to her with an umbrella to give her shelter. She stood with me beneath the umbrella and let me put my arm around her. Then she turned her face up to mine, wonderingly, and I kissed her quickly, softly on the lips. Her lips tasted of raindrops and mint. And then she left me there, so gallant in the blistering rain. She ran home laughing. But it was worth the drenching.

Another day, I heard her calling to me—'No-name, Mister No-name!'—but I couldn't see her, and it was some time before I found her, halfway up a cherry tree, her feet pressed firmly against the bark, her dhoti tucked up between her thighs.

'The cherries are not ripe,' I said.

'They are never ripe. But I like them green and sour. Will you come on to the tree?'

'If I can still climb a tree,' I said.

'My grandmother is over sixty, and she can climb trees.'

'Well, I wouldn't mind being more adventurous at sixty. There's not so much to lose then.' I climbed on to the tree without much difficulty, but I did not think the higher branches would take my weight, so I remained standing in the fork of the tree, my face on a level with Binya's breasts. I put my hand against her waist, and kissed her on the soft inside of her arm. She did not say anything. But she took me by the hand and helped me to climb a little higher, and I put my arm around her, as much to support myself as to be close to her.

~

It has been days, weeks. I have wandered everywhere, looking for her but she is nowhere. I lie awake at night, and sometimes I hear her song, and I'm convinced she's standing at the door, wanting to be brought in, and I walk out into the night, walk far, but I don't see her.

The full moon rides high tonight, shining through the tall oak trees near the window. The night is full of sounds—crickets, the tonk-tonk of a nightjar, and floating across the valley from her village, the sound of drums beating and people singing. It is a festival day. Are you singing too, Binya? And are you thinking of me, as you sing, as you laugh? I am sitting here alone, and I have no one to think of but you.

Binya...I take your name again and again—as though by saying it I can make you hear me, and come to me, walking over the moonlit mountain...

There are spirits abroad tonight. They move silently in the trees; hover about the window at which I sit; they take up with the wind and rush about the house. Spirits of the trees, spirits of the old house. An old lady died here last year. She'd lived in the house for over thirty years; something of her personality surely dwells here still. When I look into the tall, old mirror which was hers, I sometimes catch a glimpse of her pale face and long, golden hair. She likes me, I think, and the house is kind to me. Would she be jealous of you, Binya?

The music and singing grows louder. I can imagine your face glowing in the firelight. Your eyes shine with laughter. You have all those people near you and I have only the stars, and the nightjar, and the ghost in the mirror.

~

I woke early, while the dew was still fresh on the grass, and walked down the hill to the stream, and then up to a little knoll where a pine tree grew in solitary splendour, the wind going hoo-hoo in its slender branches. This was my favourite place, my place of power, where I came to renew myself from time to time. I lay on the grass. The sky in its blueness swung round above me. An eagle soared in the distance. I heard her voice down among the trees; or I thought I heard it. But when I went to look, I could not find her.

I'd always prided myself on my rationality, had taught

myself to be wary of emotional states, like 'falling in love', which turned out to be ephemeral and illusory. And although I told myself again and again that the attraction was purely physical, on my part as well as hers, I had to admit to myself that my feelings towards Binya differed from the feelings I'd had for others.

Binya represented something else—something wild, dream-like, fairy-like. She moved close to the spirit-haunted rocks, the old trees, the young grass. She had absorbed something from them—a primeval innocence, an unconcern with the passing of time and events, an affinity with the forest and the mountains, and this made her special and magical.

And so, when almost a month went by, and I did not find her on the hillside, I went through all the pangs of frustrated love: had she forgotten me and gone elsewhere? Had we been seen together, and was she being kept at home? Was she ill? Or had she been spirited away?

I could hardly go and ask for her. I would probably be driven from the village. It straddled the opposite hill, a cluster of slate-roof houses, a pattern of little terraced fields. I could see figures in the fields, but they were too far away, too tiny, for me to be able to recognize anyone.

I found a little boy on the cherry tree where I had kissed her. Had he seen a girl here, a girl who came with her cows, a girl called Binya? No one came there to graze their cows, he said.

He was lying.

Another day, two women were on the hillside, cutting grass. Had they seen a girl here, a girl who came with her cows, a girl called Binya? They told me to go back home. Too many men had heard her song and wasted away in love. She had been singing her song for a very long time, from the time before they were born. Go back home, they said.

They were lying.

And I brooded; walked disconsolately through the oak forest, hardly listening to the birds—the sweet-throated whistling thrush; the shrill barbet; the mellow-voiced doves. Happiness had always made me more responsive to nature. Feeling miserable, my thoughts turned inward. I brooded upon the trickery of time and circumstance; I felt the years were passing by, *had* passed by, like waves on a receding tide, leaving me washed up like a bit of flotsam on a lonely beach.

Then I forced myself to snap out of my melancholy. I kept away from the hillside and the forest. I did not look towards the village. I buried myself in my work, tried to think objectively, and wrote an article on 'The Inscriptions on the Iron Pillar at Kalsi'; very learned, very dry, very sensible.

But at night I was assailed by thoughts of Binya. I

could not sleep. I switched on the light, and there she was, smiling at me from the looking glass, replacing the image of the old lady who had watched over me for so long.

The Bar That Time Forgot

'Cockroaches!' exclaimed Her Highness, the maharani. 'Cockroaches everywhere! Can't put down my glass without finding a cockroach beneath it!'

'Cockroaches have a special liking for this room,' observed Colonel Wilkie from his corner by the disused fireplace. 'For one thing, our Melaram there—' and he indicated the bartender with a tilt of his double chin—'never washes the glasses properly. And there are sandwich remains all over the place. Last week's sandwiches, I might add. From that party of yours, Vijay.'

Vijay, former Test cricketer, now forty and with a forty-three waist, turned to the colonel. 'You should see the kitchen. A pigsty. The cook is seldom sober.'

'We are seldom sober,' said Suresh Mathur, income-tax lawyer, from his favourite bar stool.

'Speak for yourself,' snapped H.H. 'Simon, fetch me another whiskey.'

Simon Lee, secretary-companion to Her Highness, rose dutifully from his chair and took her glass over to the bar counter.

'Indian whiskey or Scotch, sir?' asked the bartender in a loud voice, knowing the maharani was too mean to buy Scotch.

'Whiskey will do,' said Simon. 'And a beer for me.' just then he felt like spiking the maharani's whiskey with something really lethal and be free of her for the rest of his days. Years of loyalty and companionship had given way to abject slavery, and there was nothing he could do about it. Nearing seventy, unqualified and unworldly, he could hardly set about creating any sort of career for himself.

'And what are you having?' he asked Suresh Mathur, who had just put away his first drink.

'I'm never vague, I ask for Haig!' Suresh replied, chuckling at his clever rhyme. None of the others thought it amusing, but this was usual. 'When they stop giving me credit, I'll try the local stuff.'

'Good on you!' called Colonel Wilkie from his corner. 'But there's nothing to beat Solan No. 1. Don't trust these single malts—they always give me gout!'

'I've never seen you move from that chair,' said Vijay. 'No wonder you suffer from gout.'

'Played cricket once, like you,' said the colonel. 'Made a few runs. But they always made me twelfth man. Got fed up carrying out the drinks, or fielding when the star batsman felt indisposed. Gave up cricket. Indoor games are better. Why don't we have a dartboard in here? In England, every respectable pub has a dartboard.'

I'd been listening to this conversation from a small table behind a potted palm. I was sixteen, just out of school, and I wasn't supposed to be in the bar, even if I wasn't drinking. The large potted palm separated the barroom from the outer lounge; it was neutral territory.

'I have a dartboard!' I piped up, and every head turned towards me. Most of them had been unaware of my presence. They knew, of course, that I was the son of the lady who managed the hotel.

Suresh Mathur, the most literary-inclined of the lot, said, 'Young Copperfield has a dartboard!'

'I'll go fetch it,' I said, only too ready to justify my presence in the bar.

I dashed down the corridor to my room and collided with my mother, who was doing her nightly round of the hotel.

'What are you doing here? You mustn't hang around the bar,' she said sharply. 'You have a radio in your room, apart from all your books.'

The radio had been given to me the previous year by a guest who was now wanted by the police (on suspicion of being a serial killer), but I did not feel in any way guilty about possessing it; the guest had been very friendly and generous.

'Darts,' I told my mother. 'They want to play darts. That's what a pub is for, isn't it?' and I charged into my room, picked up my old dartboard, just below a framed picture of winged cherubs sporting about on some unlikely clouds.

'Whoever gets the highest score has a free drink,' announced Vijay.

'Who pays for it?' asked Suresh Mathur.

'We all do—income-tax lawyers included.'

'He never saved anyone a rupee of tax,' declared the maharani. 'But come on, let's have a game.'

'Would you like to start the proceedings, H.H.?'

'No, I'll wait till everyone's finished. You can start with Colonel Wilkie.'

'Age before beauty,' said Vijay. 'Come on, Colonel, we know you have a steady hand.'

Colonel Wilkie's hand was far from steady. His hands were always trembling. But he struggled out of his chair and took up his position at a point indicated by Vijay. Only one of his darts struck the board, earning him fifteen points. The others were near misses. Two darts bounced off the picture on the wall.

'The old fool's aiming at those naked cherubs,' crowed H.H. 'Go on, Simon, see if you can win a free drink for me.'

Simon did his best but scored a meagre thirty points.

'Idiot!' cried H.H. 'And you always said you were a good darts player.'

'Out of practice,' Simon mumbled.

Meanwhile, someone had opened up the old radiogram and placed a record on the turntable. The cheeky voice of Maurice Chevalier filled the room:

> *All I want is just one girl,*
> But I've got to have one girl,
> *Yes, all I want is one—*
> *All I want is one—*
> *For a start!*

The evening was livening up. Suresh Mathur scored a few points, but it was Vijay who hit the bullseye and claimed a drink on the house.

'Not until I've had my turn,' shouted H.H., and made a grab for the darts.

She flung them at the board at random, missing wildly—so much so that one dart lodged itself in Colonel Wilkie's old felt hat, which was hanging from a peg, while another streaked across the room and narrowly missed the Roman nose of Reggie Bhowmik, ex-actor, who had just entered the room, accompanied by his demure little wife.

Between ex-actor Reggie and former cricketer Vijay, there was no love lost. Both middle aged and no longer in demand, they were rivals in failure. One spoke of prejudice and incompetence of the cricket selectors, the other of jealousy in the film industry and his subsequent neglect. Both lived in the past— Vijay recalling the one outstanding innings he had played for the country (before being dropped after a series of failures), Reggie living on memories of his one great romantic role before a sagging waistline and alcohol-coarsened features had led to a rapid decline in his popularity. Somehow they had drifted into the backwater that was Dehra in the 1950s.

There are some places, no matter how dull or lacking in opportunity, which nevertheless take a grip on the individual—especially the more easy-going types—and hold in thrall, rendering him unfit for life in a larger, more competitive milieu. Dehra was one such place.

The bar at Green's Hotel was their refuge and their strength. Here they could reminisce, hark back to glory days, even speak optimistically of the future. Colonel Wilkie, Suresh Mathur, Vijay Kapoor, Reggie Bhowmik, H.H.—the maharani—and Simon Lee, were all dropouts, failures in their own way. Had they been busy and successful, they would not have found their way to Green's every evening.

Reggie Bhowmik liked making dramatic entrances, but the maharani was just as fond of being the centre of attention, and wasn't about to give up centre stage to a fading actor.

'A double whiskey for Vijay!' she declared. 'He's the only one here who still has a steady hand.'

'You haven't felt my hand,' said Reggie, bearing down on her. 'You missed my nose by a whisker.'

'You'd look better with a scar running down your face,' said H.H. 'Then you might get a role as Frankenstein or the phantom of the opera.'

This touched a raw nerve, as Reggie had been having some difficulty in getting a decent role in recent months. But he snapped back: 'I'll play phantom on the condition you're cast as the fat soprano—then I shall take great pleasure in strangling you.'

'Let's change the subject,' said his wife, Ruby, always ready to pour oil on troubled waters. She moved over to Colonel Wilkie's table and asked, 'How have you been, Colonel?'

'Like an old bus—just about moving and badly in need of spare parts.'

'Well, have a beer with us—and some French fries if we can get any.'

'Cook's on strike,' said Vijay. 'Only liquid diet today.'

I saw my opportunity and piped up again from behind the potted palm. 'I can boil some eggs for you if you like!'

There was a stunned silence, broken by Suresh Mathur, who said, sounding a little incredulous, 'Young Master Copperfield can boil an egg!'

Everyone clapped, and Vijay said, 'Copperfield has certainly saved the day for us. First he produces a dartboard, and now he's about to save us from starvation. Go to it, Copperfield!'

Off I went, then, not to boil eggs—there weren't any in the kitchen—but to find Sitaram, the room boy, who was the only person of my age in the hotel. I found him in my room, listening to 'Bianca Geet Mala', the popular musical request programme, on my radio.

'We need some eggs,' I told him. 'Boiled.'

'Egg-man comes tomorrow,' he said. 'Cook finished the rest. Made himself an omelette, got drunk and took off!'

'Well, let's go down to the bazaar and buy some eggs. I've got enough money on me.'

So off we went and, near the clock tower, found a street vendor selling boiled eggs. We bought a dozen and hurried back to the barroom, where Vijay and Reggie were having a heated argument on the relative merits of cricket and football. Reggie didn't think much of cricket, and Vijay didn't think much of football.

'And what's your favourite game?' asked Ruby of Suresh Mathur.

'Snakes and ladders,' he said, chuckling, and returned to his drink.

'Boiled eggs!' I announced. 'On the house!'

Sitaram produced saucers, and distributed the eggs among the guests—two each, exactly.

'Do I have to peel my own egg?' asked the maharani querulously, staring down at the two eggs rolling about on her plate. 'Peel them for me, Simon!'

Simon dutifully cracked one of the eggs and began peeling it for her. 'Not that way, you fool. You're leaving all the skin on it.' And seizing the half-peeled egg from her companion, she flung it across the room, narrowly missing the bartender.

'Good throw!' exclaimed Vijay. 'You'd be great fielding on the boundary.'

'Better at baseball,' said Reggie.

'Snakes and ladders,' said Suresh again, now quite drunk.

Colonel Wilkie, equally drunk, gave a loud belch.

The maharani got up to leave. 'Well, I'm not going to sit here to be insulted by everyone. Come on, Simon, drive me home!' and she marched out of the room with an attempt at majesty, but tripped over the hotel cat, an ugly, striped creature who had sensed that there was food around and had come looking for it. The cat caterwauled, H.H. screamed and cursed, Reggie cheered and Suresh Mathur pronounced, 'When two cats are fighting, they make a hideous sound.'

Not to be outdone in nastiness, the maharani went up to Suresh, looked him up and down, and said, 'It's easy to tell you're a single man.'

'I'm not homosexual,' said Suresh defensively. (The word 'gay' had yet to be used in any sense other than 'happy' in those days.)

'No.' The maharani smiled wickedly. 'You're single because you are so damn ugly!'

And on that triumphant note she left the room, followed by the obedient Simon.

'Pay no attention to her, Suresh,' said Vijay generously. 'You're better-looking than that old lapdog who follows her around.'

'I understand she's leaving him her fortunes,' said Reggie. 'I could do with some of it myself. Perhaps I could interest her in producing a film.'

'She's tight-fisted,' said Vijay. 'If you look closely at Simon, you'll notice he's wearing the late maharaja's smoking jacket and deer-stalker cap. The old maharaja loved dressing up like Sherlock Holmes.'

Colonel Wilkie came out of his reverie. 'When I was in Jamnagar—' he began.

'We've heard that a hundred times,' said Vijay.

'I haven't,' said Ruby.

'When I was in Jamnagar,' continued Colonel Wilkie, 'I saw Duleepsinhji make a hundred. That was against Lord Tennyson's team.'

'Yesterday you said Ranjitsinhji,' remarked Vijay.

'I'm not that old,' said Colonel Wilkie, struggling to his feet. 'But old enough to want to go to bed. I'll toddle off now!' Locating his walking stick, he found his way to the door, wishing everyone goodnight as he passed them. They heard the tap of his walking stick as he walked away, down the corridor.

'Shouldn't someone go with him?' asked Ruby. 'It's very late and he isn't too steady on his feet.'

'Oh, he'll find his way home,' said Suresh nonchalantly. 'Lives just around the corner, in rented rooms near the Club.'

'Why doesn't he join the Club?'

'Can't afford it. Neither can I.'

'Neither can I,' said Vijay.

'Neither can we,' added Ruby, sadly. 'And anyway, it's more homely here. Even when the maharani is around.'

'She can afford the Club,' said Suresh. 'But they won't let her in. Created a disturbance once too often. Insulted the secretary and emptied a dish of chicken biryani on his head.'

'Not done,' said Vijay. 'Not cricket.'

'I don't believe it,' said Reggie. 'Can't be true.'

'Calling me a liar?' asked Suresh, bristling.

Ruby poured oil on troubled waters again. 'Interesting if true,' she said. 'And if not true, still interesting.'

'Mark Twain.'

My mother came along the corridor just as Vijay had shown off his knowledge of literature and found me behind the palms, listening to all this fascinating talk.

'Time you went to your room, young man,' she said.

'I'm waiting for everyone to go home,' I said. 'Then I'll help Sitaram tidy up. There's no cook, as you know.'

'Let him stay,' called Suresh from his bar stool. 'It's all part of his education. And he's old enough for a glass of beer. How old are you, sonny?'

'Sixteen,' I said.

'Well, enjoy yourself. It's later than you think.'

But I wasn't thinking of beer just then. I knew there were sausages in the fridge, and I had every intention of polishing them off as soon as all the guests had gone. I wanted to be a writer, but I had no intention of starving in a garret. However, all thoughts of food vanished when I looked across the room and saw Colonel Wilkie framed in the opposite doorway. He was staring at us through the glass. The glass door then opened of its own volition, and Colonel Wilkie stepped into the room. We all looked up, and Reggie said, 'Back again, Colonel? Still feeling thirsty?' But Colonel Wilkie ignored the jibe and walked slowly across the room to the table where he had been sitting. This was close to where I was standing. He bent down and picked up his pipe from the table. He'd forgotten it when he'd left the barroom. Shoving the pipe into his pocket, he turned and retraced his steps, leaving the room by the door from which he had entered.

'Well, I'm blowed,' said Vijay. 'I thought he was sleep-walking.'

'Never goes anywhere without his pipe,' said Suresh. 'A perfect example of single-mindedness.'

'Didn't say a word.'

'The pipe was all that mattered.'

'Like a favourite cricket bat,' said Vijay.

'Maybe I'll come back for mine when I'm dead.'

A silence fell upon the room. The mention of death had a sobering effect upon the small group. And come to think of it, Colonel Wilkie, on his return to the barroom, had something of the zombie about him—the walking dead.

There was a commotion in the passageway, and my mother burst into the room, followed by the night watchman.

'Colonel Wilkie's dead,' said my mother. 'He collapsed on his steps about half an hour ago.'

'But he was here five minutes ago,' said Vijay.

'No, sir,' said Gopal the watchman. 'I went home with him when he left here some time back. Madam said to keep an eye on him. When we got to his place, he began climbing his steps with some difficulty. I helped him to the top step, and then he collapsed. I dragged him into his room and then ran for Dr Bhist. He is there now.'

There was silence for a couple of mintues, and then Ruby said, 'We all saw him. Colonel Wilkie.'

'We saw his ghost,' Vijay murmured.

'He came for his pipe,' said Suresh quietly. 'I told you he wouldn't go anywhere without it.'

Colonel Wilkie was buried the next day, and we made sure his pipe was buried with him. We did not want him turning up from time to time, looking for it. It could be a bit unnerving for the customers.

In all excitement, I'd forgotten about the sausages, but decided they would keep until after the funeral.

All the regular barflies turned up for the funeral. H.H. was quite sloshed when she arrived and had to be extricated from an open grave into which she had slipped, the ground being soft and yielding after recent rain. She blamed Secretary Simon for the mishap and called him an '*ullu ka pattha*'—son of an owl—but he was quite used to such broadsides and took them in his stride. Was it love or loyalty or dependence that kept him in abeyance? Or was it, as some said, the prospect of becoming her heir? If so, he was paying a heavy price well in advance of such a prospect. Not everyone relishes being abused and kicked around in public by a half-crazed maharani.

When Colonel Wilkie's coffin was lowered into the

grave, we all said 'Cheers!' he would have liked that. We then returned to Green's for an early opening of the bar. Alcoholics Unanimous held a subdued but not too melancholy meeting.

But bad news was in store for everyone. A day or two later, I heard the owner, our Sardarji, inform my mother that the hotel had been sold and that she'd have to leave at the end of the month. She'd been expecting something like this and had already accepted a matron's job at one of the schools in the valley. As for me, I was to be packed off to England, to my aunt's home in Jersey. The prospect did not thrill me, but I was more or less resigned to it. And there did not appear to be much future for me in Dehra.

Even before the month was out, workers had begun pulling down parts of the building. It was to be rebuilt as a cinema hall, and would show the latest hits from Bombay. It was even rumoured that Dilip Kumar, the biggest star of the era, would inaugurate the new cinema when it was ready to open.

The spirit and character of a building lasts only while the building lasts. Remove the roof beams, pull down the walls, smash the stairways, and you are left with nothing but memories. Even the ghosts have nowhere to go.

An old hotel that once had a personality of its own was now dismantled with startling rapidity. It had gone up slowly, brick by brick; it came down like a house of cards. No treasures cascaded from its walls; no skeletons were discovered. In two or three days the demolishers had wiped out the past, removed Green's Hotel from the face of the earth so effectively that it might never have existed.

Searching through the ruins one day, I found a bottle opener lying in the dust, and kept it as a souvenir.

The bar had been the only common factor in the lives of those disparate individuals who had come there so regularly—drawn to the place rather than to each other.

Now they went their different ways—Suresh Mathur to the Club, the maharani to her card table and private bar, Vijay to a public school as cricket coach, Reggie Bhowmik and Ruby to Darjeeling to make a documentary... Sitaram continued to work for my mother, so I had his company whenever he was free.

The cinema came up quite rapidly, but I had left for England before it opened. When I returned five years later, it was showing Madhubala and Guru Dutt in a romantic comedy, *Mr & Mrs 55*.

Then I moved to Delhi.

Whispering in the Dark

A wild night. Wind moaning, trees lashing themselves in a frenzy, rain beating down on the road, thunder over the mountains. Loneliness stretched ahead of me, a loneliness of the heart as well as a physical loneliness. The world was blotted out by a mist that had come up from the valley, a thick, white, clammy shroud.

I groped through the forest, groped in my mind for the memory of a mountain path, some remembered rock or ancient deodar. Then a streak of blue lightning gave me a glimpse of a barren hillside and a house cradled in mist.

It was an old-world house, built of limestone rock on the outskirts of a crumbling hill station. There was no light in its windows; probably the electricity had been disconnected long ago. But if I could get in, it would do for the night.

I had no torch, but at times the moon shone through the wild clouds, and trees loomed out of the mist like primeval giants. I reached the front door and found it locked from within. I walked round to the side and broke a window-pane, put my hand through shattered glass and found the bolt.

The window, warped by over a hundred monsoons, resisted at first. Then it yielded, and I climbed into the mustiness of a long-closed room, and the wind came in with me, scattering papers across the floor and knocking some unidentifiable object off a table. I closed the window, bolted it again; but the mist crawled through the broken glass, and the wind rattled in it like a pair of castanets.

There were matches in my pocket. I struck three before a light flared up.

I was in a large room, crowded with furniture. Pictures on the walls. Vases on the mantelpiece. A candlestand. And, strangely enough, no cobwebs. For all its external look of neglect and dilapidation, the house had been cared for by someone. But before I could notice anything else, the match burnt out.

As I stepped further into the room, the old deodar flooring creaked beneath my weight. By the light of another match I reached the mantelpiece and lit the candle, noticing at the same time that the candlestick was a genuine antique with cutglass hangings. A deserted cottage with good furniture and glass. I wondered why no one had ever broken in. And then realized that I had just done so.

I held the candlestick high and glanced round the room. The walls were hung with several watercolours and portraits in oils. There was no dust anywhere. But no one answered my call, no one responded to my hesitant knocking. It was as though the occupants of the house were in hiding, watching me obliquely from dark corners and chimneys.

I entered a bedroom and found myself facing a full-length mirror. My reflection stared back at me as though I were a stranger, as though my reflection belonged to the house, while I was only an outsider.

As I turned from the mirror, I thought I saw someone, something, some reflection other than mine, move behind me in the mirror. I caught a glimpse of whiteness, a pale oval face, burning eyes, long tresses, golden in the candlelight. But when I looked in the mirror again there was nothing to be seen but my own pallid face.

A pool of water was forming at my feet. I set the candle down on a small table, found the edge of the bed—a large old four-poster—sat down, and removed my soggy shoes and socks. Then I took off my clothes and hung them over the back of a chair.

I stood naked in the darkness, shivering a little. There was no one to see me—and yet I felt oddly exposed, almost as though I had stripped in a room full of curious people.

I got under the bedclothes—they smelt slightly of eucalyptus and lavender—but found there was no pillow. That was odd. A perfectly made bed, but no pillow! I was too tired to hunt for one. So I blew out the candle—and the darkness closed in around me, and the whispering began…

The whispering began as soon as I closed my eyes. I couldn't tell where it came from. It was all around me, mingling with the sound of the wind coughing in the chimney, the stretching of old furniture, the weeping of trees outside in the rain.

Sometimes I could hear what was being said. The words came from a distance: a distance not so much of space as of time…

'Mine, mine, he is all mine…'

'He is ours, dear, ours.'

Whispers, echoes, words hovering around me with bats' wings, saying the most inconsequential things with a logical urgency. 'You're late for supper…'

'He lost his way in the mist.'

'Do you think he has any money?'

'To kill a turtle you must first tie its legs to two posts.'

'We could tie him to the bed and pour boiling water down his throat.'

'No, it's simpler this way.'

I sat up. Most of the whispering had been distant, impersonal, but this last remark had sounded horribly near.

I relit the candle and the voices stopped. I got up and prowled around the room, vainly looking for some explanation for the voices. Once again I found myself facing the mirror, staring at my own reflection and the reflection of that other person, the girl with the golden hair and shining eyes. And this time she held a pillow in her hands. She was standing behind me.

I remembered then the stories I had heard as a boy, of two spinster sisters—one beautiful, one plain—who lured rich, elderly gentlemen into their boarding-house and suffocated them in the night. The deaths had appeared quite natural, and they had got away with it for years. It was only the surviving sister's deathbed confession that had revealed the truth—and even then no one had believed her.

But that had been many, many years ago, and the house had long since fallen down…

When I turned from the mirror, there was no one behind me. I looked again, and the reflection had gone.

I crawled back into the bed and put the candle out. And I slept and dreamt (or was I awake and did it really happen?) that the woman I had seen in the mirror stood beside the bed, leant over me, looked at me with eyes, flecked by orange flames. I saw people moving in those eyes. I saw myself. And then her lips touched mine, lips so cold, so dry, that a shudder ran through my body.

And then, while her face became faceless and only the eyes remained, something else continued to press down upon me, something soft, heavy and shapeless, enclosing me in a suffocating embrace. I could not turn my head or open my mouth. I could not breathe.

I raised my hands and clutched feebly at the thing on top of me. And to my surprise it came away. It was only a pillow that had somehow fallen over my face, half suffocating me while I dreamt of a phantom kiss.

I flung the pillow aside. I flung the bedclothes from me. I had had enough of whispering, of ownerless reflections, of pillows that fell on me in the dark. I would brave the storm outside rather than continue to seek rest in this tortured house.

I dressed quickly. The candle had almost guttered out. The house and everything in it belonged to the darkness of another time; I belonged to the light of day.

I was ready to leave. I avoided the tall mirror with its grotesque rococo design. Holding the candlestick before me, I moved cautiously into the front room. The pictures on the walls sprang to life.

One, in particular, held my attention, and I moved

closer to examine it more carefully by the light of the dwindling candle. Was it just my imagination, or was the girl in the portrait the woman of my dream, the beautiful pale reflection in the mirror? Had I gone back in time, or had time caught up with me?

I turned to leave, and the candle gave one final sputter and went out, plunging the room in darkness. I stood still for a moment, trying to collect my thoughts, to still the panic that came rushing upon me. Just then there was a knocking on the door.

'Who's there?' I called.

Silence. And then, again, the knocking, and this time a voice, low and insistent: 'Please let me in, please let me in…'

I stepped forward, unbolted the door, and flung it open.

She stood outside in the rain. Not the pale, beautiful one, but a wizened old hag with bloodless lips and flaring nostrils and—but where were the eyes? No eyes, no eyes!

She swept past me on the wind, and at the same time I took advantage of the open doorway to run outside, to run gratefully into the pouring rain, to be lost for hours among the dripping trees, to be glad for all the leeches clinging to my flesh.

And when, with the dawn, I found my way at last, I rejoiced in birdsong and the sunlight piercing and scattering the clouds.

And today if you were to ask me if the old house is still there or not, I would not be able to tell you, for the simple reason that I haven't the slightest desire to go looking for it.

Listen to the Wind

March is probably the most uncomfortable month in the hills. The rain is cold, often accompanied by sleet and hail, and the wind from the north comes tearing down the mountain-passes with tremendous force. Those few people who pass the winter in the hill station remain close to their fires. If they can't afford fires they get into bed.

I found old Miss Mackenzie tucked up in bed with three hot-water bottles for company. I took the bedroom's single easy chair, and for some time Miss Mackenzie and I listened to the thunder and watched the play of lightning. The rain made a tremendous noise on the corrugated tin roof, and we had to raise our voices in order to be heard. The hills looked blurred and smudgy when seen through the rain-spattered windows. The wind battered at the doors and rushed round the cottage, determined to make an entry; it slipped down the chimney, but stuck there choking and gurgling and protesting helplessly.

'There's a ghost in your chimney and he can't get out,' I said.

'Then let him stay there,' said Miss Mackenzie.

A vivid flash of lightning lit lip the opposite hill, showing me for a moment a pile of ruins which I never knew were there.

'You're looking at Burnt Hill,' said Miss Mackenzie. 'It always gets the lightning when there's a storm.'

'Possibly there are iron deposits in the rocks,' I said.

'I wouldn't know. But it's the reason why no one ever lived there for long. Almost every dwelling that was put up was struck by lightning and burnt down.'

'I thought I saw some ruins just now.'

'Nothing but rubble. When they were first settling in the hills they chose that spot. Later they moved to the site where the town now stands. Burnt Hill was left to the deer and the leopards and the monkeys—and to its ghosts, of course…'

'Oh, so it's haunted, too.'

'So they say. On evenings such as these. But you don't believe in ghosts, do you?'

'No. Do you?'

'No. But you'll understand why they say the hill is haunted when you hear its story. Listen.'

I listened, but at first I could hear nothing but the wind and the rain. Then Miss Mackenzie's clear voice rose above the sound of the elements, and I heard her saying:

'...It's really the old story of ill-starred lovers, only it's true. I'd met Robert at his parents' house some weeks before the tragedy took place. He was eighteen, tall and fresh-looking, and full of manhood. He'd been born out here, but his parents were hoping to return to England when Robert's father retired. His father was a magistrate, I think—but that hasn't any bearing on the story.

'Their plans didn't work out the way they expected. You see, Robert fell in love. Not with an English girl, mind you, but with a hill girl, the daughter of a landholder from the village behind Burnt Hill. Even today it would be unconventional. Twenty-five years ago, it was almost unheard of! Robert liked walking and he was hiking through the forest when he saw or rather heard her. It was said later that he fell in love with her voice. She was singing, and the song—low and sweet and strange to his ears—struck him to the heart. When he caught sight of the girl's face, he was not disappointed. She was young and beautiful. She saw him and returned his awestruck gaze with a brief, fleeting smile.

'Robert, in his impetuousness, made enquiries at the

village, located the girl's father, and without much ado
asked for her hand in marriage. He probably thought
that a sahib would not be refused such a request. At the
same time, it was really quite gallant on his part, because
any other young man might simply have ravished the
girl in the forest. But Robert was in love and, therefore,
completely irrational in his behaviour.

'Of course the girl's father would have nothing to
do with the proposal. He was a Brahmin, and he wasn't
going to have the good name of his family ruined by
marrying off his only daughter to a foreigner. Robert did
not argue with the father; nor did he say anything to his
own parents, because he knew their reaction would be
one of shock and dismay. They would do everything in
their power to put an end to his madness.

'But Robert continued to visit the forest—you see it
there, that heavy patch of oak and pine—and he often
came across the girl, for she would be gathering fodder
or fuel. She did not seem to resent his attentions, and,
as Robert knew something of the language, he was soon
able to convey his feelings to her. The girl must at first
have been rather alarmed, but the boy's sincerity broke
down her reserve. After all, she was young too—young
enough to fall in love with a devoted swain, without
thinking too much of his background. She knew her
father would never agree to a marriage—and he knew
his parents would prevent anything like that happening.

So they planned to run away together. Romantic, isn't it? But it did happen. Only they did *not* live happily ever after.'

'Did their parents come after them?'

'No. They had agreed to meet one night in the ruined building on Burnt Hill—the ruin you saw just now; it hasn't changed much, except that there was a bit of roof to it then. They left their homes and made their way to the hill without any difficulty. After meeting, they planned to take the little path that followed the course of a stream until it reached the plains. After that—but who knows what they had planned, what dreams of the future they had conjured up? The storm broke soon after they'd reached the ruins. They took shelter under the dripping ceiling. It was a storm just like this one—a high wind and great torrents of rain and hail, and the lightning flitting about and crashing down almost every minute. They must have been soaked, huddled together in a corner of that crumbling building, when lightning struck. No one knows at what time it happened. But next morning their charred bodies were found on the worn yellow stones of the old building.'

Miss Mackenzie stopped speaking, and I noticed that the thunder had grown distant and the rain had lessened; but the chimney was still coughing and clearing its throat.

'That's true, every word of it,' said Miss Mackenzie.

'But as to Burnt Hill being haunted, that's another matter. I've no experience of ghosts.'

'Anyway, you need a fire to keep them out of the chimney,' I said, getting up to go. I had my raincoat and umbrella, and my own cottage was not far away.

Next morning, when I took the steep path up to Burnt Hill, the sky was clear, and though there was still a stiff wind, it was no longer menacing. An hour's climb brought me to the old ruin—now nothing but a heap of stones, as Miss Mackenzie had said. Part of a wall was left, and the corner of a fireplace. Grass and weeds had grown up through the floor, and primroses and wild saxifrage flowered amongst the rubble.

Where had they sheltered, I wondered, as the wind tore at them and fire fell from the sky.

I touched the cold stones, half expecting to find in them some traces of the warmth of human contact. I listened, waiting for some ancient echo, some returning wave of sound, that would bring me nearer to the spirits of the dead lovers; but there was only the wind coughing in the lovely pines.

I thought I heard voices in the wind; and perhaps I did. For isn't the wind the voice of the undying dead?

The Wind on Haunted Hill

Who—whoo—whooo, cried the wind as it swept down from the Himalayan snows. It hurried over the hills and passes, and hummed and moaned in the tall pines and deodars.

On Haunted Hill there was little to stop the wind—only a few stunted trees and bushes, and the ruins of what had once been a small settlement.

On the slopes of the next hill there was a small village. People kept large stones on their tin roofs to prevent them from blowing away. There was nearly always a wind in these parts. Even on sunny days, doors and windows rattled, chimneys choked, clothes blew away.

Three children stood beside a low stone wall, spreading clothes out to dry. On each garment they placed a rock. Even then the clothes fluttered like flags and pennants.

Usha, dark-haired, rose-cheeked, struggled with her grandfather's long loose shirt. She was eleven or twelve. Her younger brother, Suresh, was doing his best to hold down a bedsheet while Binya, a slightly older girl, Usha's friend and neighbour, was handing them the clothes, one at a time.

Once they were sure everything was on the wall, firmly held down by rocks, they climbed up on the flat stones and sat there for a while, in the wind and the sun, staring across the fields at the ruins on Haunted Hill.

'I must go to the bazaar today,' said Usha.

'I wish I could come too,' said Binya. 'But I have to help with the cows and the housework. Mother isn't well.'

'I can come!' said Suresh. He was always ready to visit the bazaar, which was three miles away on the other side of Haunted Hill.

'No, you can't,' said Usha. 'You must help Grandfather chop wood.'

Their father was in the army, posted in a distant part of the country, and Suresh and his grandfather were the only men in the house. Suresh was eight, chubby and almond-eyed.

'Won't you be afraid to come back alone?' he asked.

'Why should I be afraid?'

'There are ghosts on the hill.'

'I know, but I will be back before it gets dark. Ghosts don't appear during the day.'

'Are there many ghosts in the ruins?' asked Binya.

'Grandfather says so. He says that many years ago—over a hundred years ago—English people lived on the hill. But it was a bad spot, always getting struck by lightning, and they had to move to the next range and build another place.'

'But if they went away, why should there be any ghosts?'

'Because—Grandfather says—during a terrible storm one of the houses was hit by lightning and everyone in it was killed. Everyone, including the children.'

'Were there many children?'

'There were two of them. A brother and sister. Grandfather says he has seen them many times, when he has passed through the ruins late at night. He has seen them playing in the moonlight.'

'Wasn't he frightened?'

'No. Old people don't mind seeing ghosts.'

Usha set out on her walk to the bazaar at two in the afternoon. It was about an hour's walk. She went through the fields, now turning yellow with flowering mustard, then along the saddle of the hill, and up to the ruins.

The path went straight through the ruins. Usha knew it well; she had often taken it while going to the bazaar to do the weekly shopping, or to see her aunt who lived in the town.

Wild flowers grew in the crumbling walls. A wild plum tree grew straight out of the floor of what had once been a large hall. Its soft white blossoms had begun to fall. Lizards scuttled over the stones, while a whistling-thrush, its deep purple plumage glistening in the soft sunshine, sat in an empty window and sang its heart out.

Usha sang to herself, as she tripped lightly along the path. Soon she had left the ruins behind. The path dipped steeply down to the valley and the little town with its straggling bazaar.

Usha took her time in the bazaar. She bought soap and matches, spices and sugar (none of these things could be had in the village, where there was no shop), and a new pipestem for her grandfather's hookah, and an exercise book for Suresh to do his sums in. As an afterthought, she bought him some marbles. Then she went to a mochi's shop to have her mother's slippers repaired. The mochi was busy, so she left the slippers with him and said she'd be back in half an hour.

She had two rupees of her own saved up, and she used the money to buy herself a necklace of amber-coloured beads from the old Tibetan lady who sold charms and trinkets from a tiny shop at the end of the bazaar.

There she met her Aunt Lakshmi, who took her home for tea.

Usha spent an hour in Aunt Lakshmi's little flat above the shops, listening to her aunt talk about the ache in her left shoulder and the stiffness in her joints. She drank two cups of sweet hot tea, and when she looked out of the window she saw that dark clouds had gathered over the mountains.

Usha ran to the cobbler's and collected her mother's slippers. The shopping bag was full. She slung it over her shoulder and set out for the village.

Strangely, the wind had dropped. The trees were still, not a leaf moved. The crickets were silent in the grass. The crows flew round in circles, then settled down for the night in an oak tree.

'I must get home before dark,' said Usha to herself, as she hurried along the path. But already the sky was darkening. The clouds, black and threatening, loomed over Haunted Hill. This was March, the month for storms. A deep rumble echoed over the hills, and Usha felt the first heavy drop of rain hit her cheek.

She had no umbrella with her; the weather had seemed so fine just a few hours ago. Now all she could do was tie an old scarf over her head, and pull her shawl tight across her shoulders. Holding the shopping bag close to her body, she quickened her pace. She was almost running. But the raindrops were coming down faster now. Big, heavy pellets of rain.

A sudden flash of lightning lit up the hill. The ruins stood out in clear outline. Then all was dark again. Night had fallen.

'I won't get home before the storm breaks,' thought Usha. 'I'll have to shelter in the ruins.' She could only see a few feet ahead, but she knew the path well and she began to run.

Suddenly, the wind sprang up again and brought the rain with a rush against her face. It was cold, stinging rain. She could hardly keep her eyes open.

The wind grew in force. It hummed and whistled. Usha did not have to fight against it. It was behind her now, and helped her along, up the steep path and on to the brow of the hill.

There was another flash of lightning, followed by a peal of thunder. The ruins loomed up before her, grim and forbidding.

She knew there was a corner where a piece of old roof remained. It would give some shelter. It would be better than trying to go on. In the dark, in the howling wind, she had only to stray off the path to go over a rocky cliff edge.

Who—whoo—whooo, howled the wind. She saw the wild plum tree swaying, bent double, its foliage thrashing against the ground. The broken walls did little to stop the wind.

Usha found her way into the ruined building, helped by her memory of the place and the constant flicker of lightning. She began moving along the wall, hoping to reach the sheltered corner. She placed her hands flat against the stones and moved sideways. Her hand touched something soft and furry. She gave a startled cry and took her hand away. Her cry was answered by another cry—half snarl, half screech—and something leapt away in the darkness.

It was only a wild cat. Usha realized this when she heard it. The cat lived in the ruins, and she had often seen it. But for a moment she had been very frightened. Now, she moved quickly along the wall until she heard the rain drumming on the remnant of the tin roof.

Once under it, crouching in the corner, she found some shelter from the wind and the rain. Above her, the tin sheets groaned and clattered, as if they would sail away at any moment. But they were held down by the solid branch of a straggling old oak tree.

Usha remembered that across this empty room stood an old fireplace and that there might be some shelter under the blocked-up chimney. Perhaps it would be drier than it was in her corner; but she would not attempt to find it just now. She might lose her way altogether.

Her clothes were soaked and the water streamed down from her long black hair to form a puddle at her feet. She stamped her feet to keep them warm. She thought she heard a faint cry—was it the cat again, or an owl?—but the sound of the storm blotted out all other sounds.

There had been no time to think of ghosts, but now that she was there, without any plans for venturing out again, she remembered Grandfather's story about the lightning-blasted ruins. She hoped and prayed that lightning would not strike *her* as she sheltered there.

Thunder boomed over the hills, and the lightning came quicker now, only a few seconds between each burst of lightning.

Then there was a bigger flash than most, and for a second or two the entire ruin was lit up. A streak of blue sizzled along the floor of the building, in at one end and out at the other. Usha was staring straight ahead. As the opposite wall was lit up, she saw, crouching in the disused fireplace, two small figures—they could only have been children!

The ghostly figures looked up, staring back at Usha. And then everything was dark again.

Usha's heart was in her mouth. She had seen, without a shadow of a doubt, two ghostly creatures at the other side of the room, and she wasn't going to remain in that ruined building a minute longer.

She ran out of her corner, ran towards the big gap in the wall through which she had entered. She was halfway across the open space when something—someone—fell against her. She stumbled, got up and again bumped into something. She gave a frightened scream. Someone else screamed. And then there was a shout, a boy's shout, and Usha instantly recognized the voice.

'Suresh!'

'Usha!'

'Binya!'

'It's me!'

'It's us!'

They fell into each other's arms, so surprised and relieved that all they could do was laugh and giggle and repeat each other's names.

Then Usha said, 'I thought you were ghosts.'

'We thought *you* were a ghost!' said Suresh.

'Come back under the roof,' said Usha.

They huddled together in the corner chattering excitedly.

'When it grew dark, we came looking for you,' said Binya. 'And then the storm broke.'

'Shall we run back together?' asked Usha. 'I don't want to stay here any longer.'

'We'll have to wait,' said Binya. 'The path has fallen away at one place. It won't be safe in the dark, in all this rain.'

'Then we may have to wait till morning,' said Suresh. 'And I'm feeling hungry!'

The wind and rain continued, and so did the thunder and lightning, but they were not afraid now. They gave each other warmth and confidence. Even the ruins did not seem so forbidding.

After an hour the rain stopped, and although the wind continued to blow, it was now taking the clouds away, so that the thunder grew more distant. Then the wind, too, moved on, and all was silent.

Towards dawn the whistling-thrush began to sing. Its sweet broken notes flooded the rainwashed ruins with music.

'Let's go,' said Usha.

'Come on,' said Suresh. 'I'm hungry.'

As it grew lighter, they saw that the plum tree stood upright again, although it had lost all its blossoms.

They stood outside the ruins, on the brow of the hill, watching the sky grow pink. A light breeze had sprung up.

When they were some distance from the ruins, Usha looked back and said, 'Can you see something there, behind the wall? It's like a hand waving.'

'I can't see anything,' said Suresh.

'It's just the top of the plum tree,' said Binya.

They were on the path leading across the saddle of the hill.

'Goodbye, goodbye…'

Voices on the wind.

'Who said goodbye?' asked Usha.

'Not I,' said Suresh.

'Not I,' said Binya.

'I heard someone calling.'

'It's only the wind.'

Usha looked back at the ruins. The sun had come up

and was touching the top of the walls. The leaves of the plum tree shone. The thrush sat there, singing.

'Come on,' said Suresh. *'I'm hungry.'*

'Goodbye, goodbye, goodbye, goodbye…'

Usha heard them calling. Or was it just the wind?

The Chakrata Cat

Chakrata is a small hill station roughly midway between Shimla and Mussoorie. During my youth, before the road became motorable, I would trek from one hill-station to the other, sometimes alone, sometimes in company. It would take me about five days to cover the distance. I was a leisurely walker. You couldn't enjoy a hike if you felt you had to catch a train at the end of it.

At Chakrata there was an old forest rest house where I would sometimes spend the night. Don't go looking for it now. It has fallen into disuse and been replaced by a new building closer to the town.

Towards sunset, late that summer, I trudged up to the rest house and called out for the chowkidar—I forget his name. He was a grizzled old man, uncommunicative.

If you told him you had just been chased by a bear, he would simply nod and say, 'You'd better rest then. You must be tired.' Nothing about the bear!

Anyway, he opened up one of the bedrooms for me, prepared a modest meal (which I enjoyed, having eaten little all day) and offered to make a fire in the old fireplace. Chakrata can be cold, even in September, and I offered to pay for the firewood if he would fetch some. He switched on the bedroom and verandah lights and then walked to the rear of the building to fetch some wood.

That was when I saw the cat.

It was a large black cat, and it was sitting before the fireplace, almost as though expecting a fire to be lit. I hadn't noticed it entering the room, and it did not pay much attention to me, just kept staring into the fireplace. Then, when it heard the chowkidar returning, it got up and left the room.

'You have a cat?' I asked, trying to make conversation while he lit the fire.

He shook his head. 'Cats come for rats,' he said, which left me no wiser. And he took off, promising to bring a cup of tea early next morning. There was a small bookshelf in a corner of the room, and I found an old favourite, *A Warning to the Curious* by M.R. James. His haunting stories of ghosts in old colleges kept me awake for a couple of hours; then I put out the light and got into bed.

I had quite forgotten about the cat.

Now I heard a soft purring as the cat jumped on to the bed and curled up near my feet. I am not particularly fond of cats, and my first impulse was to kick it off the bed. Then I thought: 'Well, it's probably used to sleeping in this room, especially with the fire lit. I'll let it be, as long as it doesn't start chasing rats in the middle of the night!' And all it did was come a little closer to me, advancing from my feet to my knees, and purring loudly, as though quite satisfied with its situation.

I fell asleep and slept soundly. In fact, I must have slept for a couple of hours before I woke to a feeling of wetness under my armpit. My vest was wet, and something was sucking away at my flesh.

It was with a feeling of horror that I realized that the cat had crawled into bed with me, that it had now stretched out beside me, and that it was licking away at my armpit with a certain amount of relish, for the purring was louder than ever.

I sat up in bed, flung the cat from me, and made a dash for the light switch. As the light came on, I saw the cat standing at the foot of the bed, tail erect and hair on end. It was very angry. And then, for the space of five seconds at the most, its appearance changed and its head was that of a human—a woman, black-browed with flaring nostrils and large crooked ears, her lips full and drenched with blood—my blood!

The moment passed, and it was a cat's head once again. She let out a howl, left the bed, and disappeared through the bathroom door. My shirt and vest were soaked with blood. For over an hour the cat had been licking and sucking at my fragile skin, wearing it away until the blood oozed out. Cat or vampire or witch's revenant? Or a combination of all three…

I ran to the bathroom. The cat had taken off through an open window. I closed the window, bathed my wound and examined myself in the mirror.

I had not been bitten. There were no teeth marks, no scratches. The tongue, and constant licking, had done the damage.

I found some cotton-wool in my haversack, and used it to stop the trickle of blood from my armpit. Then I changed my vest and shirt, and sat down on an easy chair to wait for the dawn. It was three in the morning. I felt weak and fell asleep in my chair, to be wakened by the chowkidar knocking on my door with a cup of tea.

Chakrata is a lovely place, prettier than most hill stations, but I had no desire to linger there. There was a bus to Dehradun at eight o'clock. I decided to cut short my trek and take the bus.

'Where's that cat of yours?' I asked the chowkidar before I left. He knew nothing about a cat. Did not care for cats. They were unlucky, the companions of evil spirits, creatures of the world of the dead. I did not stop

'I'm not afraid of ghosts, Mehmoud.'

'That's because you haven't seen one. Although, I'm not sure it was a ghost. And I did not actually see anything. But I felt it all right!'

'You can't *feel* a ghost, Mehmoud. At least, not in stories.'

'This wasn't a story. It was my first night in Carpet-sahib's house in the jungle above Nainital. It was a big house with many rooms, and I was given one of my own. But there was no electricity in that out-of-the-way place. We used kerosene lamps or candles.

'I had brought my own razai and blanket, but the mattress was a strange one, and so was the pillow. It wasn't a pillow, really, but an old cushion, very hard and lumpy. It was my first night in that bed, and I was very uncomfortable. The candle burnt itself out, and I was still wide awake. I could see very little, there was just a small window allowing a little moonlight into the room. I was almost asleep when I heard someone groaning beside me. Groaning loudly, as though in pain. But there was no one else in the bed, and no one beneath it.

'The groaning stopped for a time, and then, just as I was about to fall asleep, it started again. Groan, groan, groan. Now it seemed to come from beneath my pillow.

'I turned on my side, and slowly, carefully, I slipped my hand beneath the pillow.

'It encountered a hairy face, a gaping mouth, hollow sockets instead of eyes. Horrible to touch!

'Not the face of a human, baba—the face of a rakshas!

'I tried to pull my hand away, but it was seized by that terrible mouth. A mouth with long, sharp teeth—teeth like daggers! It would have bitten my fingers off if I hadn't screamed and shouted for help.

'Carpet-sahib and his sister and the other servants came running. As they rushed into the room with torches and a lamp, those awful teeth released my hand.

'"Under the pillow!" I screamed. "Under the pillow!"

'They looked under the pillow. But there was nothing there. I showed them my fingers—they were bleeding badly.

'"A rat must have bitten you," said Carpet-sahib's sister. But she knew it wasn't a rat. And she gave me another room to sleep in.'

'And were you all right in the second room?'

'For a couple of nights, baba. Then it happened again.'

'You put your hand under the pillow again? And the face was there?'

'Not the whole face, baba. Just something soft and squishy.

'I thought it was a snail under my pillow. So I got up, lit my lamp, and looked under the pillow.'

'What was it, Mehmoud? Tell me quickly.'

'It was an *eyeball*, baba. An eye that had been removed

from its socket. It was staring up at me. Just an eyeball—staring!

'I picked it up and threw it out of the window. I threw the pillow away, too. Something terrible had happened upon that pillow, I'm sure of it.'

'So it wasn't the room?'

'It wasn't the room. It was the pillow, baba. Next day, I went into town and bought a new pillow, and from then on I slept beautifully every night. Never use a strange cushion or pillow, baba. Terrible things have happened on pillows. So remember—when you return to school next month, take a new pillow, and don't use anyone else's!'

After listening to Mehmoud's story, I was always careful to use my own pillow. Even now, many many years later, I carry my own pillow wherever I go. No hotel pillows for me. You never know what might be lurking beneath them.

A Dreadful Gurgle

Have you ever woken up in the night to find someone in your bed who wasn't supposed to be there?

Well, it happened to me when I was at a boarding school in Shimla, many years ago.

I was sleeping in the senior dormitory, along with some twenty other boys, and my bed was positioned in a corner of the long room, at some distance from the others. There was no shortage of pranksters in our dormitory, and one had to look out for the introduction of stinging-nettle or pebbles or possibly even a small lizard under the bedsheets. But I wasn't prepared for a body in my bed.

At first I thought a sleepwalker had mistakenly got into my bed, and I tried to push him out, muttering, 'Devinder, get back into your own bed. There isn't room for two of us.' Devinder was a notorious sleep-walker, who had even ended up on the roof on one occasion.

But it wasn't Devinder.

Devinder was a short boy, and this fellow was a tall, lanky person. His feet stuck out of the blankets at the foot of the bed.

It must be Ranjit, I thought. Ranjit had huge feet.

'Ranjit.' I hissed. 'Stop playing the fool, and get back to your own bed.'

No response.

I tried pushing, but without success. The body was heavy and inert. It was also very cold.

I lay there wondering who it could be, and then it began to dawn on me that the person beside me wasn't breathing, and the horrible realization came to me that there was a corpse in my bed. How did it get there, and what was I to do about it?

'Vishal,' I called out to a boy who was sleeping a short distance away. 'Vishal, wake up, there's a corpse in my bed!'

Vishal did wake up, 'You're dreaming, Bond. Go to sleep and stop disturbing everyone.'

Just then there was a groan, followed by a dreadful gurgle, from the body beside me. I shot out of bed, shouting at the top of my voice, waking up the entire dormitory.

Lights came on, there was total confusion. The Housemaster came running. I told him and everyone else what had happened. They came to my bed and had a good look at it. But there was no one there.

On my insistence, I was moved to the other end of the dormitory. The house prefect, Johnson, took over my former bed.

Two nights passed without further excitement, and a couple of boys started calling me a funk and a scaredy-cat. My response was to punch one of them on the nose.

Then, on the third night, we were all woken by several ear-splitting shrieks, and Johnson came charging across the dormitory, screaming that two icy hands had taken him by the throat and tried to squeeze the life out of him. Lights came on, and the poor old Housemaster came dashing in again. We calmed Johnson down, and put him in a spare bed. The Housemaster shone his torch on the boy's face and neck, and sure enough, we saw several bruises on his flesh, and the outline of a large hand.

Next day, the offending bed was removed from the dormitory, but it was a few days before Johnson recovered from the shock. He was kept in the infirmary until the bruises disappeared. But for the rest of the year he was a nervous wreck.

Our nursing sister, who had looked after the infirmary for many years, recalled that some twenty years earlier, a boy called Tomkins had died suddenly in the dormitory. He was very tall for his age, but apparently suffered from a heart problem. That day he had taken part in a football match, and had gone to bed looking pale and exhausted. Early next morning, when the bell rang for morning gym-work, he was found stiff and cold, having apparently died during the night.

'He died peacefully, poor boy,' recalled our nursing sister.

But I'm not so sure. I can still hear that dreadful gurgle from the creature in my bed. And there was the struggle with Johnson. No, there was nothing peaceful about that death. Tomkins had gone most unwillingly…

An Incident at the Morgue

A morgue is not a noisy place, as a rule. And for a morgue attendant, corpses are silent companions.

Old Mr Jacob, who lives just behind the cottage, was once a morgue attendant for the local mission hospital. In those days it was situated at Sunny Bank, about a hundred metres up the hill from where I now live. One of the outhouses served as the morgue; Mr Jacob begs me not to identify it.

He tells me of a terrifying experience he went through one night at the morgue.

'I was on night duty. It was a moonless night, and very quiet, but for an owl that kept hooting. It got on my nerves, so I would go out and clap loudly to drive the stupid bird away. There would be silence then, but no sooner had I come back indoors, the hooting would start again. After some time, I gave up and lit a cigarette.

'The body of a young man had been found floating in the Aglar river, behind Landour, and late that evening it had been brought to the morgue. It was placed on the table and covered with a sheet, and I wondered if it was in some way disrespectful to be smoking next to it. It was a silly thought, but it wouldn't go away, so I stubbed out the cigarette.

'You must not think I was frightened. I was quite accustomed to seeing corpses of various kinds and did not mind sharing the same room with them, even after dark. On this occasion a friend had promised to join me, and to pass the time I strolled around the room, whistling a popular tune. I think it was "Danny Boy", if I remember right.

'My friend was a long time coming, and I soon got tired of whistling and sat down on the bench beside the table. The night was very still, even the owl had gone to sleep or flown away to hunt, and I began to feel uneasy. My thoughts went to the boy who had drowned and I wondered what he had been like when he was alive. Dead bodies are so impersonal… He was probably from one of the villages higher up, he would have had a hard life toiling in those fields. Had he left old parents behind? A young wife? Children?

'The morgue had no electricity, just a kerosene lamp,

and after some time I noticed that the flame was very low. As I was about to turn it up, it suddenly went out. I lit the lamp again, after extending the wick. I returned to the bench, but I had not been sitting there for long when the lamp again went out, and something moved very softly and quietly past me.

'I felt quite sick and faint, and could hear my heart pounding away. The strength had gone out of my legs, otherwise I would have fled from the room. I felt quite weak and helpless, unable even to call out…as something, someone, began to move in the darkness.

'Presently I heard footsteps, yes they were footsteps—coming nearer and nearer. I could not move, I was afraid even to breathe. Something cold and icy touched one of my hands and felt its way up towards my neck and throat. It was behind me, then it was before me. Then it was *over* me. I was in the arms of the corpse!

'I must have fainted, because when I woke up I was on the floor, and my friend was trying to revive me. The corpse was back on the table.'

'It may have been a nightmare,' I suggested. 'Or you allowed your imagination to run riot.'

'No,' said Mr Jacobs. 'There were wet, slimy marks on my clothes. And the feet of the corpse matched the wet footprints on the floor.'

After this experience, Mr Jacobs refused to do any more night duty at the morgue. A lady replaced him, the first—and to this day, the only—lady morgue attendant in our town. I have met her on a few occasions, a charming lady who tells me she will write a book one day. She has many stories to tell, all gathered from her conversations with the corpses she watches over. Ghosts, she assures me, are far more interesting than people.

The Skull

I am not normally bothered by skeletons and old bones—they are after all just the chalky remains of the long dead—so, when my nephew Anil came back from medical college with a well-preserved skull, it was no cause for alarm. He was a second-year student, at times a bit of a prankster.

'I hope you didn't take it without permission,' I said, taking the skull in my hands and admiring its symmetry but without philosophizing upon it like Hamlet.

'Oh, the college is full of them,' said Anil. 'I just borrowed it for the vacation.' He placed it on the mantelpiece, among some of the awards and mementoes (cheap brassware mostly) that had accumulated over the years, and I must say it livened up the shelf a little.

Anil had placed the skull at one end of the mantelpiece, and there it stood until we'd had our dinner. He settled down with a book, while I poured myself a small glass of cognac before settling into an easy chair with a notebook on my knee. It was midsummer, and the window was open, so that we could hear the crickets singing in the oak trees. My cottage was on the outskirts of Mussoorie, surrounded by Himalayan oak and maple.

I had been making some notes for an article on wild flowers. When I had finished my notes and cognac, I looked up and noticed that the skull now stood in the centre of the mantelpiece.

'Did you move the skull?' I asked.

'No,' said Anil, looking up. 'I placed it at the end of the shelf.'

'Well, it's now in the middle. How did it get there?'

'You must have moved it yourself, without noticing. That was a stiff cognac you drank, uncle.'

I let it pass; it did not seem important.

~

People often dropped in to see me. Schoolteachers, visitors to the hill station, students, other writers, neighbours. During that week I had a number of visitors, and of course everyone noticed the skull on the mantelpiece. Some were intrigued, and wanted to know whose skull it was. One or two lady teachers were frightened by it. A fellow writer thought it was in bad taste, displaying human remains in my sitting-room. One visitor offered to buy it.

I would gladly have sold the wretched thing, but it belonged to Anil and he intended taking it back to Meerut. But when the time came to leave, he forgot about the skull, his mind no doubt taken up with other matters—such as the daily phone calls he received from a girl student in Delhi. After seeing him off at the bus stop, I came home to find that the skull was still occupying pride of place on the mantelpiece.

I ignored it for a few days, and the skull didn't seem to mind that. It was receiving plenty of attention from visitors during the day.

But it was beginning to get on my nerves. Every evening, when I sat down to enjoy a whiskey or a cognac, I would feel its empty eye sockets staring at me. And on one occasion, when I tried to change its position, my hand got caught in its jaw-bone and it was with some difficulty that I withdrew it.

Getting fed up of its presence, I decided to lock the thing away where it wouldn't be seen.

There was a wall cupboard in the room, where I kept my manuscripts, notebooks, and writing materials, and there was plenty of room there for the skull. So I shifted it to the cupboard, and made sure the doors were locked.

That evening I enjoyed my drink without being watched by that remnant of a human head. The crickets were singing, a nightjar was calling, and a zephyr of a wind moved swiftly through the trees. I finished my article and went to bed in a happy frame of mind.

In the middle of the night, I woke to a loud rattling sound. At first I thought it was a loose door latch or an insecure drain-pipe; then I realized the noise was coming from the wall cupboard. A rat, perhaps? But no, as soon as I opened the cupboard door, out popped the skull, landing near my feet and bouncing away right across the drawing room.

For the sake of peace and quiet, I returned it to the mantelpiece. If a skull could smile, it would probably have done so. I went back to my bed and slept like a baby. It takes more than a dancing skull to keep me from enjoying a good night's sleep.

Next morning I got to work making up a parcel. Normally I hate making parcels, they usually fall apart. But for once I took pleasure in making a parcel. I wrapped the skull in a plastic bag, then placed it in a strong cardboard box, wrapped this in brown parcel paper, used a liberal amount of sellotape, and addressed the package to Dr Anil at his medical college. Then I walked into town and handed it over to the registration clerk at the post office.

Rubbing my hands with satisfaction, I treated myself

to fish and chips and an ice cream before setting out on the walk down the hill to my cottage.

How did the skull get out of that parcel? I shall never know, perhaps a nosy postal clerk had opened it to check the contents. I hope he got the fright of his life.

Anyway, I was about halfway down the steep path that leads to one of our famous schools when I heard something rattling down the slope behind me. At first I thought it was an empty tin, but then I recognized my boon companion, that wretched skull, embellished with bits of wrapping paper and sellotape, bouncing down the hill towards me. I broke into a run, making a dash for the cottage door. But it was there before me, grinning up at me from a pot full of flowering petunias.

So back it went to its favourite place on the mantelpiece. And there it remained for several weeks.

~

The school's playing field was situated just above the path to the cottage, and during the football season I could hear the boys kicking a football around.

One day a football escaped from the field and came bouncing down the hillside, landing in a flower bed. The match was over and no one bothered to come down to retrieve the ball. But it gave me an idea. I removed the bladder, stuffed the skull into the leather interior, and tied it up firmly. Then I had the football delivered to the school's sportsmaster with my compliments.

Nothing happened for a couple of days. There was no shortage of footballs. Then in the middle of a game against St George's College, a ball went out of the grounds and a spare one was required.

The replacement didn't bounce quite as well as the previous one, and it was inclined to spin around a lot and take off in directions opposite to those intended. Also, it squeaked whenever it received a kick, and sometimes those squeaks sounded a bit like screams of protest. The goalkeepers at either end found the ball difficult to hold—it did its best to elude their grasp. And more goals were scored by accident rather than design. Finally this eccentric ball was kicked out of play and was replaced by another.

What happened to old footballs? I expect they finally fall apart and end up in a dustbin.

In this case, the football found a new owner, for the sportsmaster was a kind man who gave away old bats, balls and other worn-out stuff to the poor children of the locality. A boy from a village near Rajpur was the recipient of the battered football, and he and his friends carried it away with a cheer, kicking it all the way down the steep path, making so much noise that they did not hear the groans of protest that issued from the battered old football.

Well, weeks passed, months passed, without the skull making a reappearance. But then something strange began to happen. I found myself missing that troublesome skull!

It had, after all, been company of a sort for a lonely writer living on his own on the edge of the forest. And when you have lived with someone for a long time, then no matter how much you may quarrel or get on each other's nerves, a bond is formed, and the strength of that bond can only be known when it is broken.

The skull had been sharing my life for over a year, and now that it was gone, seemingly for ever, my life seemed rather empty.

So I began searching for the skull. I enquired amongst the children down in Rajpur; but they had long since lost the football. I made a round of all the junk shops in Dehradun, without any luck. There were lots of old footballs lying around, but not the one I wanted. And no, they didn't buy or sell human skulls.

Young Anil, the doctor, paid me a brief visit and found me looking depressed.

'What's the trouble?' he asked. 'You look as though you have just lost a friend.'

'I have, indeed,' I said. 'I miss that skull you gave me. It was company of a sort.'

'Well, I'll get you another. No shortage of skulls in my college.'

'No, I don't want another. I want the same skull. It had a personality of its own.' Anil looked at me as though he thought I was going off my rocker. And perhaps I was.

And then one day, as I was walking down a busy street in neighbouring Saharanpur, I noticed a fortune-teller plying his trade on the pavement. I don't believe in fortune-telling, but everyone has to make a living, and telling fortunes seems to me a harmless way of doing it. And then I noticed that he had a skull beside him, and that he would consult it before handing his customer a slip of paper with words on it. It looked a bit like my skull, but I couldn't be sure. All the kicking and manhandling it had received had possibly altered its appearance.

But anyway, I gave the fortune-teller some money and asked him for a prediction. He chanted something, then extracted a slip of paper from beneath the skull and handed it to me with a flourish.

I read the words printed neatly on paper.

'*Ullu ka pattha*—Son of an owl,' went the message, followed by '*Gadhe ka baccha*—Child of a donkey!' It was definitely my skull! Only an old friend could abuse me like that.

So I pleaded and haggled with the fortune-teller, paid him a hundred rupees for the skull, and carried it home in triumph.

And there it is today, decorating my mantelpiece,

a little the worse for wear, and with a silly grin on its skeletal face. To improve its looks I have placed an old cricket cap on its head.

Sometimes, we don't value our friends until we lose them.

Three in a Bed

A box-bed has many uses. It can be used to store clothes, extra bedding, old files, mementoes of past triumphs, secret stocks of gin or Scotch, even things like bedpans, enemas, and framed photographs of distant relatives. Most of the rooms in the old Royal Hotel had iron bedsteads with springs, and honeymoon couples complained that these made a lot of noise, squeaking and twanging just when the loving couple, consumed by passion, were in the throes of ecstasy. Groans and moans of pleasure don't mix well with the protests of a creaking bed. So Nandu, the owner of the Royal, decided to introduce wooden box-beds in some of the rooms, starting with Room 14.

Why Room 14? Well, it should really have been Room

13, but as hotel guests are often superstitious about the number thirteen, the Royal had decided to do away with it altogether and jump straight from Room 12 to Room 14. So Room 14 was, in fact, Room 13 under another name. You can change your name too, if you put a notice in the papers. But Nandu did not bother with such formalities. He was, in fact, thinking of adding an 'e' to Royal, in order to Frenchify it a little.

So anyway, when it came to innovating with the fixtures, Room 14 was the first room that suggested itself to Nandu, since it had already gone through a round of innovation in rechristening.

The box-bed proved to be quite a hit. It was broad and spacious and accommodated two people quite comfortably. There were no complaints from honeymooners or, for that matter, from married or unmarried couples, vintage or freshly bottled. Even single occupants appreciated the box-bed. It was surmounted by two solid but yielding Dunlopillo mattresses, and Nandu placed a pea beneath them to see if any princess would feel it, but it went undetected.

At the end of June, a newly married couple from Bombay moved into Room 14. They were very tired and went to bed early. They had been to Shimla and Kulu, and were running out of kisses and endearments. A good night's sleep was all they wanted. But it was not to be. That box-bed was playing tricks on them. It wasn't as flat as it ought to have been. There was a definite tilt to one side, and sleepy bride kept sliding off.

'This thing doesn't close properly,' said the eager bridegroom, and got up to see what was wrong with the bed. He shifted the bedclothes and lifted the lid of the box-bed. And there, staring up at them with lifeless eyes, was a comely young man, quite naked and quite dead.

Naturally, the newly-weds made a scene. It was not a part of the package, they complained, and Nandu had to agree. They were given another room with an old-fashioned spring bed and, having played their part in this story, they went to live a normal married life.

Saddled with a dead body in his best box-bed, Nandu had no option but to send for the police in the middle of the night. Two sleepy constables and a grumpy inspector arrived on the scene, as did a local doctor, who confirmed that the man in the bed was dead. But who was he and how did he get there in the first place?

~

That was the question I asked Nandu when I met him for breakfast the next morning. The body had been taken away and was now laid out on a stone slab in the civil hospital's morgue, awaiting post-mortem.

'Were there any obvious injuries?' I asked. 'Was he shot, stabbed, strangled or beaten to death?'

'Nothing at all,' said Nandu. 'No signs of violence. He looked quite peaceful and relaxed.'

'A good ad for a box-bed. But he wouldn't have crawled into the box of the bed in order to enjoy a natural death. Someone must have put him there.'

'Well, he had two companions,' Nandu said. 'They were from Hisar, all three of them. Just out of college, it seems. Having a good time.'

'So where are the other two?'

'They checked out yesterday. We presumed all three had gone. It's peak season now, and there's a lot of coming and going.'

'So perhaps they quarrelled, and he was killed in a fight, and they stuffed him into the box-bed and made a hurried exit. Did you find the clothes?'

'Yes. They were rolled up beside him.'

'That means they killed him while he was undressed. Perhaps it was the result of a sex orgy.'

'All speculation, my friend. Let's wait for the result of the post-mortem.'

But the post-mortem did not reveal much. Food, water and a fair amount of alcohol had been consumed. No signs of catalepsy or poisoning. No injuries. Death due to suffocation, or just plain respiratory failure.

The mystery would only be solved as and when the police tracked down the two companions.

This did not prove to be too difficult. The names

and addresses in the hotel register turned out to be genuine. The young men were traced to their homes in Hisar, and they admitted to having shared a room with their friend, Rohit, but said that Rohit had decided to stay back in Mussoorie instead of accompanying them back to Hisar.

Rohit's parents were contacted. Devastated by the news, they dashed up to Mussoorie to recover their son's body. They did not suspect foul play. But the police made inquiries, questioning neighbours and friends and colleagues of Rohit, and it appeared that there had been some rivalry over a girl, although this had blown over when the girl had rejected all three of them. The three friends had then driven up to the hill station to have a good time and recover from the blow to their vanity. A certain amount of alcohol had been consumed, and other guests had complained of their high-spirited antics; but if there had been a quarrel, it had not taken place in public.

The case was the talk of the town for a few days and then interest in it died down. The young men were not locals, after all, and hill-station gossip confines itself mostly to friends and neighbours. It is usually friends who give you away, and these youths were strangers without local acquaintances. The Mussoorie police left the investigation to the Hisar police, who had their suspicions but little or no evidence. And in those days there were no TV channels to pursue their own investigations.

Occasionally, I would drop in at the Royal to see my old friend Miss Ripley-Bean, who had rooms in the old wing of the building, and to listen to Mr Lobo strumming out old tunes on an out-of-tune piano, or Nandu reminiscing about the great times he'd enjoyed in Paris, when he was, so he said, something of a playboy. I would usually walk home to my cottage in Kempty village, an hour's tramp through the forest. But one evening thunder rolled over the mountains, a wind sprang up and the rain came down in torrents.

'You'd better spend the night here,' said Nandu. 'It's going to rain all night.'

'But the hotel's full,' I said. 'Mr Lobo says all rooms are taken.'

'Room 14 is vacant.'

'Isn't that where you found the body?'

'Yes. Are you superstitious?'

'No, I'm not. But I thought the room was sealed.'

'No, they've finished with it. What was there to find? No weapon, no love letters. Tourists come and go, and most of them take their problems away with them. Very selfish of these chaps to leave their friend behind, and that too in my brand new box-bed.'

'I'll be quite happy with one of your old beds,' I said.

'There's nothing wrong with the bed!' Nandu

protested. 'If a serial killer sleeps in one of our beds, does that make it an evil bed? If Marilyn Monroe sleeps in it, does it become a glamorous bed?'

'It might,' I said. 'Some people are suggestive.'

'But you are not. Have another cognac, and in the morning join me for breakfast.'

~

And so to bed, as Samuel Pepys said.

And like Pepys, I am a good sleeper. My head has only to touch the pillow and I am off to dreamland.

For in that sleep…where dreams may come…

The bed was spacious and I was able to stretch myself out and roll about at will, for I am inclined to travel a lot in my dreams. I think I was lying on a beach in Tahiti when I flung out an arm and came into contact with someone beside me.

Not the bronzed Tahitian love goddess of my dreams, but a very stiff and unyielding male torso.

In short, a corpse!

I switched on the bed lamp. Yes, there it was, right in the middle of the bed.

I leapt from the bed and switched on the overhead light.

And there, sprawled across the bedsheets, was the naked corpse of a tall, good-looking young man.

But he was there for no more than twenty or thirty seconds. The vision passed, and I was staring at an empty bed. 'Just a bad dream,' I told myself and, going to the bathroom, I switched on the light inside.

Stretched out in the marble tub, eyes vacant and jaws slack, was the naked body of the same young man.

I left Room 14 in a hurry and ran across the open forecourt to Miss Ripley-Bean's room, banging on her door and calling out to her to let me in.

As she opened her door, I was immediately attacked by her Tibetan terrier, Fluff, who took hold of my pyjamas and nearly wrenched them off. When Fluff finally recognized me and allowed me to sit down, I told Miss Ripley-Bean of my experience.

'Nothing to worry about,' she said. 'You're psychic, that's all.'

And she took out her bottle of home-made crème de menthe and gave me a hefty dose. Awful stuff, but it revived me.

Miss Ripley-Bean used the house phone to call our friend Mr Lobo, the hotel pianist, and the three of us sat down and discussed my dream, or vision, or supernatural visitation, and it was generally agreed that young Rohit had appeared to me to let us know that he had drowned in the bathtub.

'That's how they must have killed him,' opined Miss Ripley-Bean. 'One of them took him by the feet and pulled, while the other held his head under water. Death by drowning or suffocation. Fiendish! And then of course they had to hide the body, so they transferred it to the box-bed, where it wouldn't be found for a few days. But they were a bit careless with the lid, not closing it properly, as that honeymoon couple discovered.'

Miss Ripley-Bean and Mr Lobo urged me to stay for breakfast. Everyone was offering me breakfast; but I wanted to get back to my cottage in Kempty. Better a boiled egg at home than caviar in a haunted hotel.

~

Our theory was of course communicated to the police, but they made light of it. A victim returning from the dead to reveal how he had died did seem a little far-fetched, although the inspector admitted that it seemed very likely that Rohit had died in the bathtub, accidentally or by design, and that his companions had thought the box-bed would be the best place to hide the body. He promised to communicate his suspicions to the Hisar police.

Whether he did or not, we shall never know; but further action wasn't really required.

There were no cellphones in those days, but word of mouth was just as effective, and one day Nandu informed us that the former occupants of Room 14, the two youths who had left their companion behind, had been killed in a car accident while crossing the Beas River in Punjab.

The toll collector at the approach to the bridge over the river had collected the tax and issued a full receipt for it. Both he and his companion had seen the car with its two occupants drive on to the bridge, then slow down as a stark figure, apparently stark naked, walked in front of the car, hailing its occupants. The car suddenly accelerated, tried to swerve around the stationary figure, skidded, broke through the low parapet wall and plunged into the river.

Down, down it went, straight to the bottom of the river, where it came to rest on another kind of bed—a swirling riverbed.

There were two witnesses to the accident—the toll keeper and his assistant. There was no sign of the third man on the bridge.

The Monkeys

I couldn't be sure, next morning, if I had been dreaming or if I had really heard dogs barking in the night and had seen them scampering about on the hillside below the cottage. There had been a Golden Cocker, a Retriever, a Peke, a Dachshund, a black Labrador, and one or two nondescripts. They had woken me with their barking shortly after midnight, and made so much noise that I got out of bed and looked out of the open window. I saw them quite plainly in the moonlight, five or six dogs rushing excitedly through the long monsoon grass.

It was only because there had been so many breeds among the dogs that I felt a little confused. I had been in the cottage only a week, and I was already on nodding or speaking terms with most of my neighbours.

Colonel Fanshawe, retired from the Indian Army, was my immediate neighbour. He did keep a Cocker, but it was black. The elderly Anglo-Indian spinsters who lived beyond the deodars kept only cats. (Though why cats should be the prerogative of spinsters, I have never been able to understand.) The milkman kept a couple of mongrels. And the Punjabi industrialist who had bought a former prince's palace—without ever occupying it— left the property in charge of a watchman who kept a huge Tibetan mastiff.

None of these dogs looked like the ones I had seen in the night.

'Does anyone here keep a Retriever?' I asked Colonel Fanshawe, when I met him taking his evening walk.

'No one that I know of,' he said and gave me a swift, penetrating look from under his bushy eyebrows. 'Why, have you seen one around?'

'No, I just wondered. There are a lot of dogs in the area, aren't there?'

'Oh, yes. Nearly everyone keeps a dog here. Of course every now and then a panther carries one off. Lost a lovely little Terrier myself, only last winter.'

Colonel Fanshawe, tall and red-faced, seemed to be waiting for me to tell him something more—or was he just taking time to recover his breath after a stiff uphill climb?

That night I heard the dogs again. I went to the window

and looked out. The moon was at the full, silvering the leaves of the oak trees.

The dogs were looking up into the trees, and barking. But I could see nothing in the trees, not even an owl.

I gave a shout, and the dogs disappeared into the forest.

Colonel Fanshawe looked at me expectantly when I met him the following day. He knew something about those dogs, of that I was certain; but he was waiting to hear what I had to say. I decided to oblige him.

'I saw at least six dogs in the middle of the night,' I said. 'A Cocker, a Retriever, a Peke, a Dachshund and two mongrels. Now, Colonel, I'm sure you must know whose they are.'

The Colonel was delighted. I could tell by the way his eyes glinted that he was going to enjoy himself at my expense.

'You've been seeing Miss Fairchild's dogs,' he said with smug satisfaction.

'Oh, and where does she live?'

'She doesn't, my boy. Died fifteen years ago.'

'Then what are her dogs doing here?'

'Looking for monkeys,' said the Colonel. And he stood back to watch my reaction.

'I'm afraid I don't understand,' I said.

'Let me put it this way,' said the Colonel. 'Do you believe in ghosts?'

'I've never seen any,' I said.

'But you have, my boy, you have. Miss Fairchild's dogs died years ago—a Cocker, a Retriever, a Dachshund, a Peke and two mongrels. They were buried on a little knoll under the oaks. Nothing odd about their deaths, mind you. They were all quite old, and didn't survive their mistress very long. Neighbours looked after them until they died.'

'And Miss Fairchild lived in the cottage where I stay? Was she young?'

'She was in her mid-forties, an athletic sort of woman, fond of the outdoors. Didn't care much for men. I thought you knew about her.'

'No, I haven't been here very long, you know. But what was it you said about monkeys? Why were the dogs looking for monkeys?'

'Ah, that's the interesting part of the story. Have you seen the langur monkeys that sometimes come to eat oak leaves?'

'No.'

'You will, sooner or later. There has always been a band of them roaming these forests. They're quite harmless really, except that they'll ruin a garden if given half a chance… Well, Miss Fairchild fairly loathed those monkeys. She was very keen on her dahlias—grew some prize specimens—but the monkeys would come at night, dig up the plants, and eat the dahlia bulbs. Apparently they found the bulbs much to their liking. Miss Fairchild would be furious. People who are passionately fond of gardening often go off balance when their best plants are ruined—that's only human, I suppose. Miss Fairchild set her dogs on the monkeys, whenever she could, even if it was in the middle of the night. But the monkeys simply took to the trees and left the dogs barking.

'Then one day—or rather one night—Miss Fairchild took desperate measures. She borrowed a shotgun, and sat up near a window. And when the monkeys arrived, she shot one of them dead.'

The Colonel paused and looked out over the oak trees which were shimmering in the warm afternoon sun.

'She shouldn't have done that,' he said. 'Never shoot a monkey. It's not only that they're sacred to Hindus— but they are rather human, you know. Well, I must be getting on. Good day!' And the Colonel, having ended his story rather abruptly, set off at a brisk pace through the deodars.

I didn't hear the dogs that night. But the next day I saw the monkeys—the real ones, not ghosts. There were about twenty of them, young and old, sitting in the trees munching oak leaves. They didn't pay much attention to me, and I watched them for some time.

They were handsome creatures, their fur a silver-grey, their tails long and sinuous. They leapt gracefully from tree to tree, and were very polite and dignified in their behaviour towards each other—unlike the bold, rather crude red monkeys of the plains. Some of the younger ones scampered about on the hillside, playing and wrestling with each other like schoolboys.

There were no dogs to molest them—and no dahlias to tempt them into the garden.

But that night, I heard the dogs again. They were barking more furiously than ever.

'Well, I'm not getting up for them this time,' I mumbled, and pulled the blanket over my ears.

But the barking grew louder, and was joined by other sounds, a squealing and a scuffling.

Then suddenly the piercing shriek of a woman rang through the forest. It was an unearthly sound, and it made my hair stand up.

I leapt out of bed and dashed to the window.

A woman was lying on the ground, three or four huge monkeys were on top of her, biting her arms and pulling at her throat. The dogs were yelping and trying to drag the monkeys off, but they were being harried from behind by others. The woman gave another blood-curdling shriek, and I dashed back into the room, grabbed hold of a small axe, and ran into the garden.

But everyone—dogs, monkeys and shrieking woman—had disappeared, and I stood alone on the hillside in my pyjamas, clutching an axe and feeling very foolish.

The Colonel greeted me effusively the following day.

'Still seeing those dogs?' he asked in a bantering tone.

'I've seen the monkeys too,' I said.

'Oh, yes, they've come around again. But they're real enough and quite harmless.'

'I know—but I saw them last night with the dogs.'

'Oh, did you really? That's strange, very strange.'

The Colonel tried to avoid my eye, but I hadn't quite finished with him.

'Colonel,' I said. 'You never did get around to telling me how Miss Fairchild died.'

'Oh, didn't I? Must have slipped my memory. I'm getting old, don't remember people as well as I used to. But, of course, I remember about Miss Fairchild, poor lady. The monkeys killed her. Didn't you know? They simply tore her to pieces...'

His voice trailed off, and he looked thoughtfully at a caterpillar that was making its way up his walking stick.

'She shouldn't have shot one of them,' he said. 'Never shoot a monkey—they're rather human, you know...'

Topaz

It seemed strange to be listening to the strains of 'The Blue Danube' while gazing out at the pine-clad slopes of the Himalayas, worlds apart. And yet the music of the waltz seemed singularly appropriate. A light breeze hummed through the pines, and the branches seemed to move in time to the music. The record player was new, but the records were old, picked up in a junk shop behind the Mall.

Below the pines there were oaks, and one oak tree in particular caught my eye. It was the biggest of the lot and stood by itself on a little knoll below the cottage. The breeze was not strong enough to lift its heavy old branches, but something was moving, swinging gently from the tree, keeping time to the music of the waltz, dancing...

It was someone hanging from the tree.

A rope oscillated in the breeze, the body turned slowly, turned this way and that, and I saw the face of a girl, her hair hanging loose, her eyes sightless, hands and feet limp; just turning, turning, while the waltz played on.

I turned off the player and ran downstairs.

Down the path through the trees, and on to the grassy knoll where the big oak stood.

A long-tailed magpie took fright and flew out from the branches, swooping low across the ravine. In the tree there was no one, nothing. A great branch extended halfway across the knoll, and it was possible for me to reach up and touch it. A girl could not have reached it without climbing the tree.

As I stood there, gazing up into the branches, someone spoke behind me.

'What are you looking at?'

I swung round. A girl stood in the clearing, facing me, a girl of seventeen or eighteen; alive, healthy, with bright eyes and a tantalizing smile. She was lovely to look at. I hadn't seen such a pretty girl in years.

'You startled me,' I said. 'You came up so unexpectedly.'

'Did you see anything—in the tree?' she asked.

'I thought I saw someone from my window. That's why I came down. Did *you* see anything?'

'No.' She shook her head, the smile leaving her face

for a moment. 'I don't see anything. But other people do—sometimes.'

'What do they see?'

'My sister.'

'Your *sister*?'

'Yes. She hanged herself from this tree. It was many years ago. But sometimes you can see her hanging there.'

She spoke matter-of-factly: whatever had happened seemed very remote to her.

We both moved some distance away from the tree. Above the knoll, on a disused private tennis court (a relic from the hill station's colonial past) was a small stone bench. She sat down on it, and, after a moment's hesitation, I sat down beside her.

'Do you live close by?' I asked.

'Further up the hill. My father has a small bakery.'

She told me her name—Hameeda. She had two younger brothers.

'You must have been quite small when your sister died.'

'Yes. But I remember her. She was pretty.'

'Like you.'

She laughed in disbelief. 'Oh, I am nothing compared to her. You should have seen my sister.'

'Why did she kill herself?'

'Because she did not want to live. That's the only reason, no? She was to have been married but she loved someone else, someone who was not of her own community. It's an old story and the end is always sad, isn't it?'

'Not always. But what happened to the boy—the one she loved? Did he kill himself too?'

'No, he took a job in some other place. Jobs are not easy to get, are they?'

'I don't know. I've never tried for one.'

'Then what do you do?'

'I write stories.'

'Do people *buy* stories?'

'Why not? If your father can sell bread, I can sell stories.'

'People must have bread. They can live without stories.'

'No, Hameeda, you're wrong. People can't live without stories.'

Hameeda! I couldn't help loving her. Just loving her. No fierce desire or passion had taken hold of me. It wasn't like that. I was happy just to look at her, watch her while she sat on the grass outside my cottage, her lips stained with the juice of wild bilberries. She chatted away—about her friends, her clothes, her favourite things.

'Won't your parents mind if you come here every day?' I asked.

'I have told them you are teaching me.'

'Teaching you what?'

'They did not ask. You can tell me stories.'

So I told her stories.

It was midsummer.

The sun glinted on the ring she wore on her third finger: a translucent golden topaz, set in silver.

'That's a pretty ring,' I remarked.

'You wear it,' she said, impulsively removing it from her hand. 'It will give you good thoughts. It will help you to write better stories.'

She slipped it on to my little finger.

'I'll wear it for a few days,' I said. 'Then you must let me give it back to you.'

On a day that promised rain I took the path down to the stream at the bottom of the hill. There I found Hameeda gathering ferns from the shady places along the rocky ledges above the water.

'What will you do with them?' I asked.

'This is a special kind of fern. You can cook it as a vegetable.'

'It is tasty?'

'No, but it is good for rheumatism.'

'Do you suffer from rheumatism?'

'Of course not. They are for my grandmother, she is very old.'

'There are more ferns further upstream,' I said. 'But we'll have to get into the water.'

We removed our shoes and began paddling upstream.

The ravine became shadier and narrower, until the sun was almost completely shut out. The ferns grew right down to the water's edge. We bent to pick them but instead found ourselves in each other's arms; and sank slowly, as in a dream, into the soft bed of ferns, while overhead a whistling thrush burst out in dark sweet song.

'It isn't time that's passing by,' it seemed to say. 'It is you and I. It is you and I…'

I waited for her the following day, but she did not come.

Several days passed without my seeing her.

Was she sick? Had she been kept at home? Had she been sent away? I did not even know where she lived, so I could not ask. And if I had been able to ask, what would I have said?

Then one day I saw a boy delivering bread and pastries at the little tea shop about a mile down the road. From the upward slant of his eyes, I caught a slight resemblance to Hameeda. As he left the shop, I followed him up the hill. When I came abreast of him, I asked: 'Do you have your own bakery?'

He nodded cheerfully, 'Yes. Do you want anything—bread, biscuits, cakes? I can bring them to your house.'

'Of course. But don't you have a sister? A girl called Hameeda?'

His expression changed. He was no longer friendly. He looked puzzled and slightly apprehensive.

'Why do you want to know?'

'I haven't seen her for some time.'

'We have not seen her either.'

'Do you mean she has gone away?'

'Didn't you know? You must have been away a long time. It is many years since she died. She killed herself. You did not hear about it?'

'But wasn't that her sister—your other sister?'

'I had only one sister—Hameeda—and she died, when I was very young. It's an old story, ask someone else about it.'

He turned away and quickened his pace, and I was left standing in the middle of the road, my head full of questions that couldn't be answered.

That night there was a thunderstorm. My bedroom window kept banging in the wind. I got up to close it and, as I looked out, there was a flash of lightning and I saw that frail body again, swinging from the oak tree.

I tried to make out the features, but the head hung down and the hair was blowing in the wind.

Was it all a dream?

It was impossible to say. But the topaz on my hand glowed softly in the darkness. And a whisper from the forest seemed to say, 'It isn't time that's passing by, my friend. It is you and I…'

Would Astley Return?

The house was called Undercliff because that's where it stood—under a cliff. The man who went away—the owner of the house—was Robert Astley. And the man who stayed behind—the old family retainer—was Prem Bahadur.

Astley had been gone many years. He was still a bachelor in his late thirties when he'd suddenly decided that he wanted adventure, romance and faraway places. And he'd given the keys of the house to Prem Bahadur—who'd served the family for thirty years—and had set off on his travels.

Someone saw him in Sri Lanka. He'd been heard of in Burma around the ruby mines at Mogok. Then he turned up in Java seeking a passage through the Sunda

Straits. After that the trail petered out. Years passed. The house in the hill station remained empty.

But Prem Bahadur was still there, living in an outhouse.

Every day he opened up Undercliff, dusted the furniture in all the rooms, made sure that the bedsheets and pillowcases were clean and set out Astley's dressing-gown and slippers.

In the old days, whenever Astley had come home after a journey or a long tramp in the hills, he had liked to bathe and change into his gown and slippers, no matter what the hour. Prem Bahadur still kept them ready. He was convinced that Robert would return one day.

Astley himself had said so.

'Keep everything ready for me, Prem, old chap. I may be back after a year, or two years, or even longer, but I'll be back, I promise you. On the first of every month I want you to go to my lawyer, Mr Kapoor. He'll give you your salary and any money that's needed for the rates and repairs. I want you to keep the house tip-top!'

'Will you bring back a wife, sahib?'

'Lord, no! Whatever put that idea in your head?'

'I thought, perhaps—because you wanted the house kept ready…'

'Ready for me, Prem. I don't want to come home and find the old place falling down.'

And so Prem had taken care of the house—although there was no news from Astley. What had happened to him? The mystery provided a talking-point whenever local people met on the Mall. And in the bazaar the shopkeepers missed Astley because he had been a man who spent freely.

His relatives still believed him to be alive. Only a few months back a brother had turned up—a brother who had a farm in Canada, and could not stay in India for long. He had deposited a further sum with the lawyer and told Prem to carry on as before. The salary provided Prem with his few needs. Moreover, he was convinced that Robert would return.

Another man might have neglected the house and grounds, but not Prem Bahadur. He had a genuine regard for the absent owner. Prem was much older—now almost sixty and none too strong, suffering from pleurisy and other chest troubles—but he remembered Robert as both a boy and a young man. They had been together on numerous hunting and fishing trips in the mountains. They had slept out under the stars, bathed in icy mountain streams, and eaten from the same cooking-pot. Once, when crossing a small river, they had been swept downstream by a flash flood, a wall of water that came thundering down the gorges without any warning during the rainy season. Together they had struggled back to safety. Back in the hill station,

Astley told everyone that Prem had saved his life while Prem was equally insistent that he owed his life to Robert.

This year the monsoon had begun early and ended late. It dragged on through most of September and Prem Bahadur's cough grew worse and his breathing more difficult.

He lay on his charpai on the veranda, staring out at the garden, which was beginning to get out of hand, a tangle of dahlias, snake-lilies and convolvulus. The sun finally came out. The wind shifted from the south-west to the north-west and swept the clouds away.

Prem Bahadur had shifted his charpai into the garden and was lying in the sun, puffing at his small hookah, when he saw Robert Astley at the gate.

He tried to get up but his legs would not oblige him. The hookah slipped from his hand.

Astley came walking down the garden path and stopped in front of the old retainer, smiling down at him. He did not look a day older than when Prem Bahadur had last seen him.

'So you have come at last,' said Prem.

'I told you I'd return.'

'It has been many years. But you have not changed.'

'Nor have you, old chap.'

'I have grown old and sick and feeble.'

'You'll be fine now. That's why I've come.'

'I'll open the house,' said Prem and this time he found himself getting up quite easily.

'It isn't necessary,' said Astley.

'But all is ready for you!'

'I know. I have heard of how well you have looked after everything. Come then, let's take a last look around. We cannot stay, you know.'

Prem was a little mystified but he opened the front door and took Robert through the drawing-room and up the stairs to the bedroom. Robert saw the dressing-gown and the slippers and he placed his hand gently on the old man's shoulder.

When they returned downstairs and emerged into the sunlight Prem was surprised to see himself—or rather his skinny body—stretched out on the charpai. The hookah was on the ground, where it had fallen.

Prem looked at Astley in bewilderment.

'But who is that—lying there?'

'It was you. Only the husk now, the empty shell. This is the real you, standing here beside me.'

'You came for me?'

'I couldn't come until you were ready. As for me, I left *my* shell a long time ago. But you were determined to hang on, keeping this house together. Are you ready now?'

'And the house?'

'Others will live in it. But come, it's time to go fishing...'

Astley took Prem by the arm, and they walked through the dappled sunlight under the deodars and finally left that place for ever.

Behind the Wall

In the late 1960s, I came to live in Mussoorie, which hadn't yet become the popular hill station that it is today. I was a struggling writer, surviving on the meagre fees I received from magazines and newspapers for my stories. But it was possible in those days to find cheap accommodation in Mussoorie—for the amount you would pay for a single room in Delhi or Bombay, you could rent one of the old cottages belonging to the British residents who had left after 1947, selling their properties for a song. These buildings were usually in bad shape, with bits and pieces falling off in different corners every other day, but at least you had a roof over your head. Indigent writers cannot be choosers!

And there were compensations. To wake at dawn and watch the rosy glow of approaching daybreak before the sun stroked its way over the mountains was a never-ending delight. In the cottage I rented there was a window seat looking out upon a sociable gathering of trees; maple, oak, rhododendron, long-leaved pine—providing a recreation ground for long-tailed blue magpies, bulbuls, minivets and the occasional paradise flycatcher—and here I spent the mornings, turning out stories, poems, essays, children's tales, anything that came to mind, some of these compositions bringing in a few cheques from time to time.

I was entirely on my own, eating out of tins and occasionally taking a meal at a dhaba near the bus stand. I went for long walks, and some of these walks took me up to the heights of Landour or down to the vale of Barlowganj or out to Happy Valley, where the Tibetan refugees had been resettled.

Barlowganj, once the property of a long-forgotten General Barlow, was now a straggling bazaar on the old Kipling Road, leading down past several large estates and princely villas—summer homes for the rich and famous. These buildings were empty for most of the year. Some of them had survived for over a century, and some of the names too—'Seven Oaks' (the original owner must have come from Kent), 'Arundel' (shades of Sir Walter Scott), 'Wynberg' (a South African connection) and 'Bala Hissar' (once the residence-in-exile of an Afghan king).

Some way below the ramparts of Bala Hissar was a quaint rambling building that went by the name of 'Hollow Oak'. I stopped at its iron gate one day and peered over, trying to see if there were any giant or hollow oaks on the premises. There were none. Perhaps they had been done away with to make room for more buildings. But trailing over the old stone wall was a branch of wisteria, its heady perfume pervading the vicinity. In the garden two children were playing—a slim boy who must have been thirteen or fourteen and a girl of ten or eleven. The girl was on a swing, singing to herself. The boy sat on a stone bench. While the girl looked pretty and vivacious, the boy had a sullen, brooding beauty, accentuated by the shifting shadows of maple leaves which played about his face.

The oaks were in new leaf, their tender milky green catching the soft late-afternoon sunlight, while the Japanese maples were sending out leaf buds, orange turning to red. The boy looked up at me, his eyes in the sunlight an unusual shade of green, sheltered by long, dark lashes. He had been cutting pictures out of a magazine. Intent on the work, he gave me no more than a glance. The girl saw me but took no notice. She was used to seeing strangers at the gate.

I have always enjoyed the company of children, being an overgrown child myself, and I was in need of friends, having lived alone for too long. Perhaps I should call out to them, I thought, strike up a conversation. But they were so happily absorbed in themselves that I felt like an intruder, so I waved to no one in particular and continued on my walk.

That evening, growing restless, I went to the cinema. In those days, before television entered every home, people went to the pictures, and the hill station boasted of at least five cinema halls, albeit small theatres. The Picture Palace was showing a slapstick comedy, an amalgam of silent shorts featuring Buster Keaton, Harry Langdon, the Keystone Kops, and my old friends Laurel and Hardy. I loved these comic geniuses of another era, and though I was a little late for the evening show, I slipped in and took a seat about midway down the hall. Already a bit short-sighted, I avoided the more expensive seats at the back. The seats up front were in poor shape, very uncomfortable, and often infested with fleas, but at least they gave me a clear view of the action on screen.

As much as I was enjoying the picture, the customer on the seat just in front of me was enjoying it even more. He giggled, laughed out loud, squirmed in his seat, even jumped up and down with delight whenever the custard pies started flying, as they did with increasing frequency. Those custard-pie fights were always great to watch—the timing was perfect, complete anarchy transformed into ballet, as everyone on the set entered into the spirit of the thing, flinging pies in all directions.

When the lights came on I found that my fellow connoisseur of silent comedy was just a boy—the same boy I had seen in the Barlowganj garden earlier that day.

He passed me on his way out, and gave me a conspiratorial smile—as though to say, 'You shared in my happiness. I heard your laughter too.'

~

Later that week, I was invited to a party at Hollow Oak, and I discovered the host was Neena, the former Maharani of Mastipur, whom I had known briefly some years ago. I hadn't met her since, and now here she was, dancing with a bottle of wine balanced on her head as loud rock music bounced off the walls.

Neena, happily sozzled, kissed me on the cheeks like a long-lost friend, and even as the bottle of wine fell off her head and shattered on the floor—which did not appear to bother anyone—she introduced me to a tall and handsome man in his forties standing next to her.

'Meet Ricardo,' she said, putting a hand on his arm in a gesture of ownership. 'He's from Bolivia.'

'Ricardo Montalban, cultural attaché in the Bolivian Embassy,' the man said, extending his hand.

I shook his hand and told him I was a writer.

'And my wife is a reader! You must meet her.'

I was introduced to the wife. Mrs Montalban was not

half as glamorous as the diplomat. She wore glasses; little or no make-up; a dress more suitable for office than a party. Almost as though she wanted to go unnoticed. By contrast, her husband was flashy, the Latin extrovert, the Valentino type, oozing sex appeal. It was clear to me that the Maharani and Ricardo were lovers. The Maharani, I remembered, could never resist a good-looking man.

Mrs Montalban could not have been ignorant of the affair; even at the party, her husband and Neena made no effort to conceal it. They were locked in embrace, dancing to a slow number, but I saw no trace of anger or anxiety on Mrs Montalban's face; she appeared unusually calm.

'I would love to read your books,' she said.

I told her there were only two, and one of them was for children.

'My daughter reads a lot,' she said. I followed her gaze to the top of the stairwell, where two children sat crouching, watching the proceedings—the same children I had seen before in the garden.

'Anna is running a slight fever, she'll be in bed soon. Pablo can come down if he wants to, but he's shy.'

'That's a nice name he has.'

'We named him after Picasso, but it's Anna who paints.'

'And what does Pablo do?'

'Dreams,' she laughed.

And just then Neena grabbed me by the arm and dragged me to the bar at the far end of the room.

I observed that it was well stocked with the choicest of wines and spirits.

'All thanks to Ricardo,' Neena said.

'Is he staying some time?'

'Only a week. Then we're off to Nepal for a month.'

'His family too?'

'No, just Ricardo and me. His family can stay in Hollow Oak, I'm hardly here. This place is dead; I like it in Delhi.'

'Don't they live in Delhi, if he's with the embassy?'

'Ricardo does, thank god!' Neena giggled. 'The wife prefers the hills. She would, the frump. She'll put the children in that school next door. Suits me; they're rich, I'll earn a good rent!'

Ricardo passed us at that moment and Neena went after him like a hungry tigress.

An ornate wall clock struck midnight, but the drinking and dancing continued. There was no sign of any dinner. Neena could sustain herself on a purely liquid diet, and so could most of her guests. But I was growing hungry. I looked around for snacks but even the peanut bowls were empty.

Mrs Montalban must have noticed, because now she was beckoning me from the next room.

She put a plate of cutlets in my hands. 'I can see

you're hungry,' she said. 'You'd better have some of the children's dinner.'

'Where are they?'

'They've eaten and gone to bed. Plenty of mutton cutlets left. You eat mutton?'

'Everything,' I said. 'Desperate writers can't be fussy.'

'Nor can desperate housewives,' she said, and helped herself to a cutlet. She seemed a homely sort of person, and I warmed to her.

'I think I'll slip away,' I said, 'but I hope to see you again.'

I wished her goodnight and left the house by the kitchen door, walking around the building and through the garden—or what had once been a formal, ornamental garden. It had been neglected for some time. Bright moonlight shone on untrimmed rose bushes and paths that were a tangle of ivy and irises gone wild.

The strident dance music followed me for some way before being dissipated by the enveloping silence of the mountains.

~

Mrs Montalban and the children had everything they wanted, but they were ill at ease in Hollow Oak. Neena's caretaker, an unsmiling nun called Sister Clarissa, who was her dead husband's hire, was in charge of the house, looking after the expenses and ordering the servants about, and making Mrs Montalban and the children feel unwelcome. This I learned from Pablo, who began to spend a lot of time with me, and I was glad of his company.

The school admissions hadn't come through yet. Anna would be busy painting landscapes all day. Pablo, hands in pockets, whistling cheerfully, would be loafing about on the Mall, drifting in and out of the cinema halls, a habit he continued even after we met.

We often met at the Rialto. It turned out we were both fans of action-filled westerns and comedies. We exchanged notes on our favourite Hollywood actors. He liked Clint Eastwood, who had recently arrived on the screen with the 'spaghetti' western. I mentioned Gary Cooper and Buster Keaton, but he was too young to have heard of them. This was before the coming of the video or internet, so there was no way of catching up with the classics.

While the films were on, Pablo rarely took notice of me. He was totally absorbed in the on-screen action, even clapping his hands when the big gunfights or custard-pie fights climaxed to his satisfaction. There was something very innocent, even old-fashioned, about his enthusiasm. It reminded me of a performance of Peter Pan, which I had seen at a London theatre in the 1950s. When Tinker Bell was dying, the audience was told she could be saved only if the audience declared that they believed in fairies. Everyone clapped—or almost everyone—and Tinker Bell was saved. Not that the audience really believed in fairies. But they went along with the spirit of the play.

Outside the hall, Pablo would come up to me and ask, 'Did you like the movie?'

'Loved it,' I would say to please him.

One day, after we had watched a re-run of *Gunfight at the O.K. Corral*, he said to me, 'The gunfight was great, wasn't it?'

'Super.'

'Did you like Wyatt Earp or Doc Holliday?'

'Both.'

'Doc Holliday drank too much. Like my father. And the Maharani.'

'She can drink more than Doc Holliday. And she's a better shot with a rifle.'

He smiled, gazing at me in a conspiratorial way. He had beautiful green eyes. His complexion was olive. His hair was black and glossy, his long hands full of gestures, his voice musical, as yet unbroken.

'Do you think they would give me a poster?' he asked unexpectedly.

I was amused. And sympathetic. I remembered my lonely boyhood expeditions to various cinemas, sometimes in out-of-the-way places—Chandni Chowk,

Meerut, even the suburbs of London—and the care and enthusiasm with which I would collect publicity leaflets, film magazines, postcards of favourite stars.

Mr Ahuja, the manager of the Rialto, was sitting in his office. I went up to him and asked, 'Do you have a spare poster that you can give this boy? He's a regular customer.'

He looked up and smiled. 'We've used them all up for this picture. But here are the posters for our next attraction. It will run for a week. *My Fair Lady*.'

'Do you like musicals?' he asked Pablo.

'He likes posters,' I said.

The manager laughed. 'Well, I can spare one, I think. Since you're regulars.' He rolled up a fairly large wall poster and handed it to me. I handed it to Pablo. He was thrilled. He took my hand and kissed it.

'I'll put it up on my bedroom wall,' he said.

The manager was touched. 'I'll save some posters for you,' he said. 'Keep coming to the Rialto.'

We assured him that we would.

And we did, going for all the shows Pablo wanted to see. One evening, it was dark by the time we reached the Hollow Oak gates. Pablo's mother was pacing up and down the garden path.

'Thank you for walking home with him,' she said, obviously relieved to see us. 'Sometimes he starts dreaming and gets lost. Would you like to come in?'

'Another time,' I said.

'After the next picture,' said Pablo. 'You'll come with me, won't you?'

'If your mother agrees.'

'Pictures, pictures,' she said. 'That's all he lives for. And there are five cinemas in town!'

'But if you are on holiday, what does it matter?'

Pablo was so pleased to have an ally in me that he broke into Spanish as he said goodnight: '*Buenas noches. Adios, amigo!*'

And one fine day Pablo was at my door, bearing a gift. He unrolled a poster, and there stood Laurel and Hardy, as large as life, in a film called *The Flying Deuces*.

'Saw it when I was a boy,' I said.

'It's being shown again,' he said. 'You told me you liked Laurel and Hardy, so I got this for you.'

'Stan and Olly forever!'

'It's showing tomorrow.'

'Then we'll see it together. How many posters do you have now?'

'Seven.'

'Mr Ahuja is very generous.'

'My mother sent him a cake.'

'Fair exchange.'

'But I have a problem, amigo.'

'What's that?'

'I can't put them up anywhere. Sister Clarissa is in

charge while the Maharani is away and she says we can't have film posters stuck all over the walls. Not even in my room.'

'Mean old thing. A few posters would brighten up the place—better than having mounted tiger heads and deer antlers suspended from the walls. We should pull them all down!'

'We can hardly move about indoors, she's so fussy. Won't let us touch the furniture. Nothing must be moved.'

'When does the Maharani come back?'

'Don't know. Sister won't say.'

'Doesn't your father phone?'

He shook his head. There was anger in his eyes, which soon turned to heart-breaking sadness.

'Come, I'll walk home with you.' And to cheer him up, I added, 'We'll take a longer route, through the forest. We might even spot a tiger!'

'We won't shoot it,' he said.

'No, we'll wrestle with it!'

His face lit up with a smile.

~

When the Maharani returned to recover from her amorous exertions with Ricardo, Mrs Montalban and her children became a nuisance. She wanted them out of the way. At the same time, she wanted to have Ricardo visiting from Delhi as often as possible, and for that reason it was important to keep his family nearby. So Sister Clarissa was instructed to find a cottage for the family, not far from Hollow Oak.

A cottage was found, badly in need of repair and restoration. It would be at least a month before it could be occupied. As for school, it was already midterm and admissions were kept pending. Pablo's extended holiday would be extended even further.

He clapped his hands gleefully. 'You can teach me at home,' he said. 'You will be my tutor, all right? We will see lots of pictures!'

'We'll have to cut down on the pictures,' I said. 'More nature walks. That way you'll learn some botany and arithmetic.'

It was the beginning of innumerable walks. Sometimes they ended up at one of the cinemas, but most of the time we covered quite a lot of ground, taking in Cloud's End, the Haunted House and the ruins of Colonel Everest's house, all at the hill station's extremities. Not many cars in those days, not many motorable roads either, so we did a lot of trudging, stopping at small inns and tea shops to sustain ourselves with boiled eggs, old buns and biscuits, and sweet, milky tea.

One day we ended up at an extensive cemetery, and I took Pablo down a winding path, amongst old graves, some of them going back well over a hundred years. The lettering had worn off most of the slabs, but had lasted better on some of the more upright tombstones—most of them British graves from the colonial era.

Hundreds of graves—the city of the dead—all reminders of our frail hold on this life and the oblivion into which we must pass. The famous, the humble, the wicked, the innocent, the ancient, the infant, struck down at random, sometimes in the midst of a busy life, sometimes when it had hardly got started…

> *Sceptre and crown must tumble down*
> *And in the dust be equal made*
> *With the poor crooked scythe and spade.*

I remembered these lines from a poem I'd learnt at school, but I couldn't remember the name of the poet. I spoke them aloud for Pablo's benefit, but he wasn't listening.

'The angel has lost her head,' he said, pausing in front of a small statue of a winged angel carved out of granite. The head was indeed missing. As were the heads and limbs of other statuary in the cemetery. Somebody had been collecting angels' heads. Even the odd wing!

'This one has only one wing, how will she fly?'

'Angles were invented before aeroplanes,' I said. 'Now that everyone can fly, who needs angels? Science hasn't left us with much to believe in.'

Pablo sat down on the grass and said, 'I'm tired. What are you looking for, amigo?'

'Nothing,' I said. 'Just contemplating the void.'

'The void?'

'The emptiness. The futility of it all. The yearning, the struggle, the desire, the loving, the hating. And it all ends here, or on the funeral pyre. Dust or ashes.'

'*Finis. Kaput.*'

'You heard that in a movie,' I said.

'But Alan Ladd doesn't die.'

'He died last month.'

'But we can still see his movies.'

'True enough. There's immortality, after all, courtesy Hollywood! So enough of graves and worms and epitaphs, let's go to the pictures.' I took his hand and pulled him to his feet.

We saw *Butch Cassidy and the Sundance Kid*, and walked home singing 'Raindrops keep falling on my head'.

~

Mrs Montalban moved into her new abode without any fuss or bother, engaged a cook and maidservant, and directed all her energies into caring for her children. In other words, she was the ideal wife and mother.

So, while Neena played the femme fatale and Montalban fancied himself as Valentino, Mrs Montalban was simply a homely bread-and-butter woman who busied herself baking cakes and cookies.

And she baked them well, as I discovered one morning when I dropped in at Pablo's invitation a week or two after they had moved into their new abode.

Already, the wide veranda looked like no veranda I had ever seen. The walls were festooned with film posters, all assiduously collected over the summer months. Apart from the manager of the Rialto, Pablo had made friends with the projectionist at the Picture Palace, the ticket seller at the Majestic, and the tea-stall owner at the Jubilee—all of whom had gone out of their way to save posters for him. Partly it was due to his personal charm and friendly nature; partly due to his generosity with his mother's cakes and cookies.

And now, on my first visit to the rented house, I was taken from one poster to another as though I were the chief guest at a grand art exhibition—which is what it was, in a way. Pablo, proud and happy, held my hand and asked, 'What do you think, amigo?'

'You are a genius, my little friend.'

I became a frequent visitor to their new house. One afternoon, I found Pablo on the front veranda. He was holding a doll, and he was busy sticking drawing pins into various part of its anatomy. When I went closer, I noticed 'MAHARANI' written in bold letters across the front of the doll.

'Drawing pins won't work,' I said. 'You need something with greater penetration.'

He wasn't put out by my intrusion.

'I've got a hammer and nails,' he said, his eyes lighting up. 'Or I could take out all the stuffing.'

'Anna wouldn't like that. Disembowelling her favourite doll.'

'It's not her favourite doll. The Maharani gave it to her on her last birthday in Delhi, but Anna doesn't come anywhere near it. Actually, she's not into dolls. Prefers ghosts.'

'Ghosts?'

'She keeps seeing a little girl who wants to play with her.'

'Have you seen her?'

He shook his head; a lock of hair fell across his brow, giving him a tender, innocent look. Not the sort who would practise voodoo on dolls.

'Only Anna has seen her.'

'Perhaps she's a real girl, but very shy. And she runs away, liked a frightened gazelle.'

'The old mali says the house is haunted.'

The mali was an eighty-year-old gardener who did odd jobs at various houses on the hill side. According to him, all the old houses were haunted.

'And what else does he say? That someone died here in tragic circumstances?'

'Yes. He doesn't say in what circumstances, only that someone died. He's sure the girl died here sometime before we moved in.'

'Most people die at home, you know. It would be hard to find an old house which hasn't been witness to a death or two. Why aren't hospitals haunted, have you thought about that? People die in them every day.'

'Maybe ghosts don't like hospitals. My mother says some people like to return to their old homes from time to time, but they won't go back to a hospital.'

'She's right. Hospitals are scary places—even for ghosts!'

As the evening wore on, Pablo took out his guitar and began strumming it without actually settling into a tune.

'Play something simple,' I said.

And for the first time I heard him singing. It was an old lullaby—something out of Africa, I think. I put it down in words that I remember, for he sang it first in Spanish and then in English:

> *How can there be a cherry without a stone?*
> *How can there be a chicken without a bone?*
> *How can there be a baby with no crying?*
> *How can there be a story with no ending?*
>
> *And then the answer to this gentle riddle:*
> *A cherry when it's blooming, it has no stone,*
> *A chicken when it's hatching, it has no bone,*

A baby when it's sleeping has no crying,
A story of 'I love you' has no ending…

'You sing better than you play,' I said. 'You must sing more often.'

He began singing another song, softly, in Spanish, and presently we were joined by Anna and Mrs Montalban. She poured me a glass of red wine and placed a currant cake before me. Normally I wasn't a wine drinker, but it went well in that house and in that company.

The sun went down with a lot of fuss. First a fiery red, and then in waves of pink and orange as it slid beneath the small clouds that wandered about on the horizon. The brief twilight of northern India passed like a shadow over the hills. I had stepped outside to watch the sunset. Now a lamp came on in the sitting room, followed by the veranda light. An atmosphere of peace and harmony descended on the hillside.

Pablo was calling me. 'Amigo, come quickly! Pronto, pronto!' Whenever he was excited, he broke into Spanish.

I stepped back into the sitting room to find him pointing at the far wall.

A faint glow had spread across the whitewashed wall, as though a part of that spectacular sunset had been left behind. And emerging from this suffused light, as through a rent in the clouds, was the face of a girl. Old-fashioned, sad-happy, beautiful.

'It's her!' exclaimed Anna. 'I've seen her at the window sometimes. And now she's *inside*!'

'She means no harm,' said Mrs Montalban, as composed and unruffled as always. 'She wants to be back here, she longs to be with us—a happy family.'

And it *was* a happy family, in Ricardo Montalban's prolonged absence.

But the face on the wall soon faded, returned to its own eternal twilight. Who was she, and why had she come back? Perhaps Mrs Montalban was right, and the girl longed to be of this world again.

We would never know—until and unless we joined her.

~

Years have passed, I have forgotten much, but I can still recall that time, that summer of long ago, and I see before me the pale, beautiful face of Pablo. His long fingers (more artistic than his sister's), the green of his eyes reflecting the morning sun, his soft, sensual lips, and one of those rare smiles which brought out the dimples in his cheeks.

Sometimes, with the rain on my face, I remember the rain on our faces when we were caught in a sudden storm, walking back from the pictures to Barlowganj— no umbrellas, his futile efforts to keep his latest poster from getting wet. We stopped at my lonely cottage and I wrapped him in a large towel, and he sat on my bed shivering while I made him a mug of strong coffee. He was an ugly duckling, all ribs and sharp bones, but with the promise of becoming a swan one day.

He smoothed out the poster and gazed tenderly at the sodden image of Elvis Presley—not exactly my poster boy, but a teenage heart-throb in his time.

'It will dry out,' I said.

He looked up and smiled at me—not with the same tenderness that he had bestowed on Elvis, but with the affection that comes from trust and companionship…

Pablo, my friend. I may stop loving you, but I will never stop loving the days I loved you…

Our parting was not a sentimental one. Early that winter, Ricardo Montalban was transferred to the Bolivian Embassy in Indonesia. The children were excited at the prospect of living in a different country. Mussoorie was, after all, a dull sort of place for young children, unless you wanted no greater excitement than walking in the hills or consuming ice creams on the Mall.

Still, Pablo showed his genuine regard for me by making me a present of all his film posters.

The day before they left, the old mali came down the path to my cottage with a large bundle containing nearly all the posters Pablo had collected—some fifty to sixty, all neatly folded and well preserved. I put them away in a cupboard. I wasn't going to turn my cottage into the foyer of a cinema hall. But I was touched by the gesture. I knew that he treasured his collection— and he felt that they would be safe with me. So Clint Eastwood, Marilyn Monroe, John Wayne, Elizabeth Taylor, Dharmendra and Meena Kumari all found their way into my cupboard (and there they would stay for many years, safe, untouched).

Departure day arrived, and I joined the Montalbans in the taxi that took us down to the railway station in Dehra. I had known the Montalbans for less than a year, but I was already feeling a part of the family. Those who have no family of their own soon grow attached to welcoming families, no matter how imperfect they may be. One has to belong somewhere. But families were always going away and leaving me behind.

I did not think I would see Pablo again, but I put on a brave face, held his hand, and bade him a cheerful goodbye.

'See you in Jakarta,' I said. 'Or even in La Paz.'

He murmured the last line of his little song, 'A story of "I love you" has no ending,' and kissed my hand. The train drew out, and he vanished from my life.

I returned to Mussoorie, to the secluded old cottage with its broken windows and sighing wind and the occasional mysterious whispers in the night.

One evening that December, the sunset stretched right across the horizon, a river of molten light, changing from marigold to pomegranate red to crimson. Before it set, the sun threw a shaft of golden light across my study wall, and there I saw the face, or rather the profile, of my friend Pablo. And he smiled briefly in my direction, fading with the dying sun.

A message, a premonition? Or just a whisper of lost friendship? The world is smaller than we think. We are all parts of one another, meeting, separating, meeting again, looking for our severed halves, heedless of time and distance…

Neena telephoned some weeks later. In the middle of other news, she told me that Ricardo had come back into her life via a long letter, although she wished he hadn't. She did not know what to do with grieving men, she said, and Ricardo was grieving. His son had drowned off the coast of Bali early that month when the family was on a holiday.

I did not go to the pictures after that, and some years later, Mussoorie's cinema halls were shut down.